She needed him inside her

She was fixated on it, waiting breathlessly for him to take her. She needed it badly. Now.

His fingers danced between her thighs, then retreated to stroke her backside, each intimate touch sending another shock wave reverberating through her. His tongue swirled into the shallow cup of her belly button. Even that was intense and erotic.

"It's okay," Rory said, pushing to her elbows. "I'm ready. You can—uh…you know."

Tucker looked up, his expression as taunting as his fingers. "Tell me."

She did. Two words that left nothing to the imagination. No sense in being coy about it.

"I'll get to that," he promised, "soon enough."

"But you must be hurting by now. I know I am."

He smiled tightly. "Let me take this trip my way. The slow, scenic route."

"Whatever you like. But don't say I didn't offer."

His hot-as-sin gaze traveled down her body. "Darling, there's no missing your open invitation."

Dear Reader,

Do you believe in fate? I often wonder how couples that were "meant to be" find each other. Fate's got to play a part. But if that's so, what happens when fate is fiddled with? Or was that also meant to be? Hmm...

Tucker and Rory, the fated couple in the third book of the LOCK & KEY trilogy, come together at a key party, where random matches are the name of the game. Or maybe not. <g> With this book I wanted to explore a different type of falling in love. Not love at first sight, but a slower realization that relies on an attraction of minds and personalities as well as physical heat. Though there's no lack of that, for certain!

I hope you enjoy traveling with Tucker and Rory on their *Slow Ride* to love.

Carrie Alexander

Books by Carrie Alexander

HARLEQUIN BLAZE

*Sex & Candy

CARRIE ALEXANDER
Slow Ride

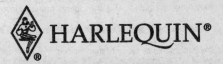

HARLEQUIN®

TORONTO • NEW YORK • LONDON
AMSTERDAM • PARIS • SYDNEY • HAMBURG
STOCKHOLM • ATHENS • TOKYO • MILAN • MADRID
PRAGUE • WARSAW • BUDAPEST • AUCKLAND

For my key partners, Jamie and Shannon,
with thanks and appreciation. Working with
two of my favorite writers was a true pleasure!

ISBN 0-373-79178-X

SLOW RIDE

1

"WANT TO SLIP IT TO ME?" a sultry, spray-tanned blonde said to Tucker Schulz at the crowded entrance of Clementine's. When he paused, astonished, she giggled and leaned over to shimmy her breasts against his arm. "Your key, silly boy." Her shiny lips puckered as she ran her hand over his midriff. "Mmm…to start with, anyway. Nice abs."

He realized that he was supposed to insert his key into the locket nestled between her cleavage and his biceps. This would entail prying his hand out of the pocket of the black denim jeans that had suddenly grown tight.

"I'll catch you later," he said to the willing blonde, strangely unwilling himself. The meat market at the Marina dance clubs wasn't his usual scene. Then again, neither was turning women down.

"Remind me again why I'm here," he shouted to his old friend, Nolan Baylor, as they entered the hot, pulsing atmosphere of the high-decibel party. Clementine's, a popular nightclub that featured gold-rush decor juxtaposed with a contemporary dance floor, was packed with a shrill crowd of young, single and trendy San

Franciscans. Tonight's event was a charity key party. The expectation of sexual chemistry was so thick in the air Tuck could taste it in the back of his throat.

"See there, at three o'clock?" Nolan nudged Tucker with his elbow. Their eyes followed the swaying mini-skirt of a Chinese enchantress whose slim hips could probably talk dirty in five languages. "*That's* why you're here. The hot babes."

Beneath his breath, Tuck whistled appreciatively. "Nope, that's why *you* are here. But wasn't it supposed to be one hot babe in particular?"

Nolan nodded. "Doesn't hurt to look."

"It'll hurt plenty if Mikki catches you." Tuck chuckled as a server skimmed by with a tray of used glasses. "The phrase 'balls on a platter' comes to mind."

Nolan took the familiar ribbing with a wry grin. On a mission to find his ex-wife, Mikki Corelli, he'd donated a small fortune to the charity's building fund to guarantee the reunion via the supposedly random matching of locks and keys guests had received at the door as they'd turned in their tickets.

"Unlock the Possibilities" was the theme for the evening. Tuck fingered the small key he'd shoved into his jeans' pocket. He'd rather be opening a cold beer and kicking back to watch the Giants play the Mariners, but when a buddy needed a wingman....

"Did you wear a cup?" he asked, thinking of Mikki and the stilettos she favored.

Nolan placed a defensive hand over his fly. His laugh wasn't altogether convincing. "You'll have to be my bodyguard."

"No way. I'm not getting between you and Mikki on this one." Nolan planned to tell the hot little mama whom he'd married during law school that their quickie Mexican divorce decree had crumbled like a cheap tortilla. Her explosion might rock harder than the Northridge earthquake.

"You do have my sympathy," Tuck added as they pushed deeper into the crowd. One zap of Mikki Corelli's electric-blue eyes could shock a man to the core, even when he wasn't delivering unwelcome news.

But that was Nolan and Mikki. They were meant for each other, even if their love-hate relationship was too tempestuous for Tuck's taste.

Keeping his dealings with women at a flirtatious level was his preference, one that had worked out fine for him ever since he'd been fifteen and asked his very first blonde to come for a ride. Surfboards, motorbikes, convertibles...himself. Any conveyance would do, as long as the coupling was fast and sweet.

He was thirty-two now, which added up to seventeen years of fast rides.

Sweat sprang up on the nape of Tucker's neck. He pulled at the collar of the nancy-boy purple silk shirt his older sister Didi had forced on him. Either he was too old for this game or the weekly—sometimes daily—haranguing of his four siblings was finally getting to him. Happily married one and all, they thought Tuck's life wouldn't be complete until he was, too. And they weren't shy about airing their opinions and advice.

They'd already been successful at luring him into a

permanent address. Several of the family had invested in an apartment building that he managed and lived in while completing the lengthy renovation process.

Marriage was the logical next step; Didi was pressing the charms of her single friend Charla hard. If Tuck wasn't careful about what bed he hopped into, one of these mornings he'd wake up to find himself fully settled down with a wife beside him and a passel of kids in the next room.

Nolan stopped short. "There she is."

Tucker gazed past his friend, who was clad in a black polo shirt that might do as a shroud after Mikki got her hands on her once-and-present husband.

"Go on. Make your move." Tuck pressed a knuckle into the small of Nolan's back. The man could talk circles around opposing counsel in court. Facing the lash of Mikki's sharp tongue and hot temper shouldn't faze him.

But she just might knock him out of his designer loafers, at least temporarily.

Mikki's dark head had snapped up. She turned slightly away from a small table crowded with drinks and food, ignoring her two companions as her eyes locked with Nolan's. Tucker watched with interest. Either a head-to-head challenge or spontaneous combustion was in the offing.

Nolan's features had tensed. "She's as beautiful as ever," he said under his breath.

"Gorgeous," Tuck agreed. Personally, he was partial to blondes, but there was nothing on Mikki that he'd say no to—if she hadn't been claimed by his best friend from the moment that the two had met in law school.

Nolan strode over to the table, radiating such an intense heat that the crowd parted in front of him. A small white-gold key had appeared in his hand.

Tuck followed. He knew exactly what would happen when that key made its way to Mikki's lock, but he still wanted a ringside seat for the show.

"What the hell are you doing here?" she snapped.

"Nice to see you again, too, Mikki." Wisely, Nolan slipped the key back into his pocket. He'd always been a man to pick his moments, as opposed to Tucker, who took things as they came.

While the pair struck at each other like flint and steel, Tucker glanced over at the two women at Mikki's table. Her sisters, according to Nolan. Foster sisters, in fact, which explained their presence to support the cause of Maureen Baxter's transitional halfway house. Both wore the suitcase locket on a chain around their necks, symbolic of the disrupted lives of the troubled teenage girls Maureen Baxter aimed to help.

"You remember Tuck," Nolan was saying in a tone that betrayed his need for a temporary buffer from Mikki's ire.

Mikki's scowl was replaced with a generous smile. She and Tucker had always been friendly, even when he'd had to stand by his man Nolan during their rancorous split.

She climbed down from her perch on the stool and gave him a heartfelt hug. In the next minute she was introducing him to her sisters.

The first one's name was lost in the din. His eyes slid past her to the other as Mikki said, "And this is Lauren

Massey." He nodded as she continued. "Tucker Schulz. He and Nolan have been friends for…"

"More years than I care to keep track of," Tuck said, deciding that seventeen years of brotherly bonding and flirtatious females was just about right, after all. He flashed a devil-may-care grin at the blonde.

Lauren was a slim woman with a froth of honey-colored curls, prettily dressed in sleeveless peach silk. More his type than the other sister, but after a brief hello she made her excuses and departed. He'd missed his shot at trying his key on her.

Tucker shrugged. Easy come, easy go. He eyed the abandoned stool, well in range of the sparks that Mikki and Nolan were still striking off each other. Mikki was trying to leave, and if the fierce light in Nolan's eyes was any indication, he wasn't about to let her go without a fight.

Good for him. Tuck slid into place, snagged a server to request a beer, then remembered the brunette sister remaining at the table, a glass of white wine in front of her. She was the eldest, he recalled. A hippie like her mother, according to Nolan. If so, she'd forgotten to sign up for the retro-issue love beads and headbands.

Tucker gave her a quick once-over. Curved wings of nut-brown hair framed her calm face. She had a strong nose and jaw, paired with a wide mouth painted a shiny plum color. Even sitting, he could see that she was tall and comfortably built—statuesque, he guessed. There was a casual but well-taken-care-of air about her that spoke of salons and designer labels.

Generally he preferred women who romped on the

beach without a care in the world. But there was something about Mikki's sister. The longer he looked, the more he liked. He found himself drawn to her bare arms and hands, struck by the elegance of her long fingers, the graceful turn of a wrist beneath a heavy silver bangle. Instinct told him she'd be good with her hands, talented with her fingers. He could easily imagine her sliding them across his body....

She lifted the glass of wine. One eyebrow arched.

He nodded. "I'm sorry. I missed your name."

She tilted a haughty chin at him. "Aurora Constable. But you can call me Rory."

He leaned closer to hear. Her voice was low and smooth, soothing among the high-pitched shrieks of the other women. "What kind of a name is Aurora?" he asked, raising his voice above the live band playing an eclectic mix of jazz, swing and pop.

"From the Aurora Borealis. Northern Lights. My mother claimed she saw them over Woodstock on the night I was conceived, but I have my doubts. Woodstock, colored lights dancing in the sky, sex that was an out-of-body experience..." Rory shrugged, then caught her shawl from slipping down her arms. "You do the math."

He grinned. "At least you got an interesting story out of it. A genuine Woodstock baby. Don't think I've ever met one."

"Oh, many make the claim, but few are the genuine article. My mother's been known to tell a few wild tales. This one I believe. My birthdate proves it, although I was born on a commune in Oregon. We didn't come to California until I was six." She stopped and bit her lip. "I'm talking too much. Sorry."

"No problem." He scanned the crowd. Couples were quickly pairing off as keys found their way to the matching locks. The flirtatious procedure was producing much laughter and raunchy banter. He could have been off among them, searching for his soul mate for the night, but he'd been raised with manners. For now, he'd stick with Rory.

"What about you?" She pushed a plate of pastries toward him. "Try one."

He picked up a cream puff drizzled with chocolate. "I'm a native Californian. Lived here all my life."

"That's rare, too."

"My parents have been in the same big Victorian for as long as I can remember. They raised five of us there. Now the bedrooms are mostly empty, but they fill them up with grandchildren as often as possible."

She glanced at his hand. "You're not married."

He shook his head and took another bite of the pastry. A dollop of filling squirted into his mouth. Rich and smooth—like Rory.

He swallowed. "None of the kids are mine. I'm the only holdout."

"At least you're an uncle." Rory's face softened with longing. She had that tender look in her eyes, the mushy one his sister Jenny got when she was cradling her pregnant belly and thinking about soon being able to hold her newborn.

A look like that, even from a woman he barely knew, would usually have Tucker running for the exit. But

Rory was only remotely an option. Attractive, in her own way, but not his type. Despite the expert hands.

"How many nieces and nephews?" she asked.

"Eight and counting."

"Aw, wonderful. A big family."

"You must know what that's like. Mikki used to tell me stories about life at Emma Constable's. There was a constant stream of foster kids coming and going, she said. Wasn't Maureen Baxter even one of them?"

"She wasn't with us for long, but we've stayed in touch." Rory glanced at the commingling singles, the set of her mouth betraying a trace of discomfort. "That's why I'm here, to help get Baxter House up and running. Not to—" she waved a hand "—unlock the possibilities."

"I figured as much." Tucker's gaze lingered on a Britney clone baring her bikini wax in a pair of low-slung jeans. "You don't seem like the type."

Rory blinked. "What type would that be?"

"You know. On the make."

The brow inched upward again. She was going all high and mighty on him. "But you are, I take it?"

He smiled. "I'm young, male and single."

"Of course." She toyed with the locket around her neck, wrapping the delicate chain around the tip of one finger and swinging the suitcase charm back and forth. Her shawl had shifted, revealing the loose neckline of her dress and a hint of the shadowed hollow between her breasts.

Full ones, he realized. Round and weighty, the kind of breasts a guy could roll and grip and squeeze and suck—

Damn. Although it wasn't unusual for him to have sexual thoughts about most any eligible woman he met, these lustful reveries were making him uneasy. Nolan was like a brother, which made Rory a…well, not a sister, but maybe a cousin. Not by blood, of course. Only by association. Still, it'd be less complicated if he didn't have impure thoughts about her.

Blame the swinging locket. No degree in psychology was necessary to deduce that she was offering him an invite, if only subconsciously.

Insert your key, her amber eyes seemed to say. *I'll take you on an a wild ride you won't forget.*

Tucker put his hand into his pocket, intending to withdraw the key. How could it hurt?

Before he could follow through, a man came up and leaned over Rory's chair, sliding his hands along her arms. He was big, muscled, bald, sporting a white button-down shirt with a loosened tie and an ostentatious platinum watch that must have weighed a couple of pounds. "Hello, lovely lady. Waiting for me?"

Rory's face tilted up. After a beat, she smiled provocatively. Tuck couldn't tell if she knew the guy or not, but he was surprised at her willingness to flirt so openly.

Maybe he should have acted faster.

With an airy laugh, Rory offered the man her locket. "All packed and ready to go, as soon as I find the matching key."

The man tapped the suitcase charm. "Let's see what you've got in there."

Rory swiveled on the stool and allowed Big Baldy to try his key on her necklace. It didn't turn.

"Just my luck," the guy said.

She dropped the necklace back into her cleavage and rearranged her shawl, crisscrossing it over one of the most magnificent pair of real breasts Tuck had ever hoped to see. "Maybe next time."

Big Baldy shot an assessing glance at Tucker before he addressed Rory again. "Want to come with me, anyway? I promise…" He lowered his face nearer to hers and whispered into her ear.

She laughed, but with less playfulness. Her eyes went to Tucker. "Thanks, but no thanks."

Tuck cocked two fingers at the man, flicking them in a shooing gesture. "Okay, fella. You took your shot. Now you're out of here."

The guy straightened. "The lady can make up her own mind."

"And she did."

There was a moment of challenging silence, then Big Baldy shrugged. "Her loss." He faded into the crowd, smoothing a hand over his shining scalp as he went.

Tuck waited until the joker was well away before he gripped the edge of the round table and leaned across it toward Rory. "What did he say to you?"

Her lashes lowered. "Oh, just something about making himself fit."

Tuck saw red. He forced himself to pry his fingers from the table and tear off a hunk of the pastry. After he'd chewed as if the flaky crust had been composed of nail filings, he swallowed and was able to say almost casually, "Do you know him?"

She shook her head. "Not really, though I'm fairly sure he's been in my bakery a few times." Her gaze on Tuck's face was level. Frank. She didn't seem to be a woman who played games. "It was nice to be asked. My only other option so far was a semifamous actor who was making the rounds earlier. Pint-size—I could have broken him like a twig."

Tuck was a solid five-eleven, one-eighty-five. Not bulky like the bald man, but he worked out. He would match up with Rory just fine. Maybe his imagination was tricking him, but he was beginning to sense a simmering heat beneath her cool exterior. She was an intriguing female.

Unfortunately, after her remark about how nice it was to be asked, pulling out his key now would look like a pity attempt.

Tuck popped the rest of the cream puff into his mouth. "You have a bakery?" Nolan may have mentioned that, now that he thought of it.

"Several of them, all local. Lavender Field. Bread and sweets. That's one of my pastries you're gobbling."

He swallowed. "Good stuff."

"Thanks."

The music stopped. They looked at each other, finding nothing further to say.

Tuck wiped his mouth with a napkin. He scanned the club from the etched-glass mirror behind the bar to the velvet curtains forming the private dining alcoves. Glass doors opened onto a deck with a sparkling view of the harbor. "Looks like Nolan went after Mikki."

"I saw her heading outside."

"What happened to your other friend?"

"My sister—Lauren. She's probably circulating, collecting quotes for a freelance article she's researching." Again, the direct gaze. "Did you want to go find her? I saw you looking."

"That's okay." Under the focus of Rory's unblinking stare, Lauren's face had faded from his memory.

"She's very pretty, isn't she?"

"Yeah, sure."

"Not as up-front as Mikki, but she's single and available." Rory shifted on the bar stool, the hem of her long cotton dress lifting to reveal a smooth firm calf as she recrossed her legs.

"Are you trying to set us up?"

"I can, if you're interested."

"Not right now." Suddenly his mouth was dry and the key was burning a hole in his pocket.

After a momentary silence the music started up again. Should he ask her to dance? The tempo was fast; the dancers were rocking. There was no doubt in his mind that Rory Constable was strictly a slow-dance woman.

"You're fidgeting," she said. "It's all right if you want to leave." Another hand wave. "Go. Circulate. Search for cute locks." She gave him a doting smile. "You know you want to."

"No." He drained his beer in one long pull. "What I want is a dance. Are you game?"

She pressed a hand to her chest and batted her lashes, putting on, just a bit. "Me?"

"Yes." He held out his hand. "*You.* Come on."

Her hand fit snugly in his and she swung off the stool, giving him a peep down the neckline of her dress to the locket dangling between her breasts. Heat throbbed through him, in beat with the music.

As he led Rory to the dance floor, he had to remind himself one more time that she wasn't his type. She was Mikki's sister; he was Mikki's husband's best friend. They were destined to be friends who met up now and then at backyard barbecues or family birthday parties. They would drink a beer together and maybe share a moment when they remembered the night that they might have hooked up, if the dice had rolled another way.

Actually hooking up would make future encounters too awkward. He'd been down that road before, with a good friend of Didi's who to this day shot diamond-cutting laser eyes at him whenever they ran into each other at his sister's house.

But one dance wouldn't hurt.

Rory was surprisingly carefree on the dance floor. For all his certainty that she was a slow-dancing type, she moved fluidly to the samba beat of "Hot, Hot, Hot," the skirt of her black-and-white patterned dress swinging in a bell shape around her long legs as she swooped and twirled.

He finally managed to catch her close, keeping one arm firmly looped around her waist so she couldn't slip away. He looked into her eyes. Their hips swiveled, side to side, forward and back.

Rory's cheeks glowed, bathed in the hot colored lights. She licked her lips. "You're a good dancer."

"Only when the mood strikes."

"The mood," she repeated. Her eyes were liquid, the color of the expensive brand of Scotch he used to see in decanters at Nolan's house.

He spread his fingers over the small of her back. Her hips moved just beneath them, the swell of her backside inches away. If he'd been even a little bit drunk and she hadn't been quite so classy, he'd dip lower for a quick grope.

"Then the elusive mood must have struck," she said, moving her face closer to his so he could hear. "I haven't danced like this since…I can't remember when."

Her hair brushed the side of his cheek. He closed his eyes, inhaled a fragrance of sweet sage and lavender. The weight and warmth of her generous body was more arousing than he'd expected.

He could sink into her.

Go deep, get comfortable.

Spend the night.

Maybe even longer…

He tightened their embrace until her voluptuous breasts were riding plump and full up against his chest, the locked charm trapped between them. In heels, she was almost his height. Maybe twenty-five pounds under his weight, which meant that her curves fit just right against him, filling his arms, his senses.

Their palms slid together in the heat. Rory panted in his ear. He'd stopped hearing the music, but the beat was inside him, and in her, too. He felt it in the heft of her soft breasts and the sensuous sway of her hips and the glide of their feet, perfectly in sync.

He touched his lips to her warm cheek. She turned her head away a fraction and his kiss slipped toward her ear. He lipped her lobe, making the dangly earring swing against his chin. His nose nudged it aside as he sought her neck, sleek and moist and infused with the rising scent of aroused female flesh. He nuzzled, he kissed, he licked.

Rory's hand tightened against his. "Tucker." She pressed her face against his shoulder and let out a soulful moan. "Sweet mercy. What are you doing to me?"

2

"FOREPLAY," Tucker said against her neck. The hot whisper of breath and the vibrations of his voice produced a frisson that played through Rory like fingers running scales along the keys of a piano.

Foreplay. On the dance floor. Was he nuts?

If so, she was equally crazy from the heat. She didn't want him to stop.

"Foreplay," she echoed, trying to regain her senses. "Are you asking—or stating your intentions?"

His lips stopped mid-nibble. "Do I need intentions?"

"Everyone has intentions."

"Not the kind that a father brings up with his daughter's boyfriend."

"Oh." Slowly, she was coming out of the haze of arousal that had freed her inhibitions more thoroughly than a half-dozen body shots. A method she'd tried only once, in college, and promptly thrown up in a frat boy's lap. "Don't worry. I wasn't asking you to marry me."

Tucker chuckled. He gave her waist a squeeze—a friendly squeeze.

When had his hand moved from her derriere to her waist?

Ignoring the signs, she stayed in his arms, resting her chin on his shoulder and attempting to find the beat of the music that had previously come so natural and easy. But Tucker's body was stiff against hers, and not in a good way.

He stepped back. "Thanks for the dance."

Her mouth hung open. That was it?

"I'm sorry about—you know." He gave a shock of his thick dark brown hair a self-conscious tug, leaving it in ruffled disarray. There was an easy charm about him that was boyishly self-effacing. She imagined that he was the kind of man who got away with murder by flashing his grin at the woman he'd wronged, a grin made only more irresistible by the deep, dimpled grooves it cut into his cheeks. Lost in that charm and smile, a woman would find herself forgiving any transgression.

"Sorry about what?" she said, giving him no easy out. If a guy was going to grope her on the dance floor and then run away, he could at least do her the courtesy of *not* apologizing.

"Getting carried away." His feet shuffled. The grin had become sheepish. "I shouldn't have been so forward."

She followed him to the edge of the dance floor, grateful to be out of the revolving lights. "Please don't look at me that way. I'm not your maiden aunt."

"No, but we're practically cousins."

Inhaling, she straightened. "I don't *think* so."

"Maybe not." Tucker's gaze went to her breasts. She fumbled around, gathering up the lilac shawl she'd let trail across the dance floor, but in the end she resisted the impulse to cover herself. She was working on her body issues—had even progressed to posing for her Friday afternoon life-drawing class—and she would not allow Tucker Schulz to see how badly he'd rattled her composure. Even if her nipples were so hard they felt like hitchhiker's thumbs sticking out the front of her dress.

Begging for a pickup, she thought with an inner groan. *Pick me up and take me on a long, slow, sensuous journey.*

"Nolan and Mikki…" Tucker's raspy voice trailed off. His gaze was still pinned below her neck and a small thrill went through her when he licked his lips. His eyes were the eerie green underwater color of the turtle tanks at the aquarium, reflecting more than his reluctance. He wanted her, but he didn't.

"What about Nolan and Mikki?" A lame excuse, in her estimation. He knew it and was using them, anyway, as a convenient out.

Tucker looked away. "I'll leave that up to her to tell you, but the upshot is that you and I—" He broke off, serving up another helping of the appealing grin-and-shrug. "We're better off as friends."

"If that," she said.

Surprised by her resistance, he caught her hand. "Aw, Rory. Don't be like that."

Despite herself, she melted. Not difficult when he'd already reduced her to a liquid state.

She kept her face solemn. "Tell me. Does the boyish charm always work when you're prying yourself out of a sticky situation?"

He was no longer fooled by her stern tone. "Pretty much."

She laughed and gave him a push. "Go on. Get out of here."

He half turned, then threw another dimple shot over his shoulder. "Friends, right? I can tell—we're destined to be good friends."

"Sure. That'd be just great."

Story of my life. Idly she twined the necklace chain around one finger, holding the charm in her palm as Tucker made his getaway. He was immediately snared by a curvaceous redhead in blue spangles who was offering him her locket before they'd gone three steps.

Unlock the possibilities? More like unlock the door of your place or mine.

The white-gold suitcase charm in her palm achingly reminded her that though she may have spruced up her outsides with the help of new designer clothes and a gym membership, inside she was still locked in the same old pattern, lugging the same old baggage.

She sighed. For a brief moment Tucker had seen her as a beautiful, desirous woman, but she'd ruined that with her insistence on keeping his intentions candid and aboveboard. As well as her failure to believe in her own attractiveness.

Almost ten years had gone by since Bradley Carr, her long-term boyfriend from college, had dumped her mere days from the altar, simply because he'd caught sight of some wannabe Bo Derek while taking the trolley. After the wedding had been canceled, the girl and Brad had used his and Rory's honeymoon tickets to Cozumel.

That they'd suffered Montezuma's revenge and broken up on the plane trip home was Rory's only small vindication.

Since then she'd resolved innumerable times that she would not let one bad relationship affect the rest of her life. The statute of limitations for feeling sorry for herself was up and over and o-u-t, *out*.

Rory looked around the club, seeing size twos everywhere.

Affirmation time. *I am a confident, successful woman with great skin and va-va-voom curves. I don't need a man to complete me, but someday I will find one to appreciate me.*

Just not at a key party.

AN HOUR LATER the charity event was on its downward slide to that time when those still hanging on to their locks and keys had to either match up or call it a night. Rory had put in her time and was ready to go, but she had Mikki's car keys and there was no way she'd leave her sister to her own devices, especially when the man who'd broken her heart was on the premises. Tucker's hints about the couple had roused Rory's curiosity. So far, Mikki had managed to dodge all questions, slipping off to the bar to order another drink whenever Rory brought up Nolan's name. Extremely worrisome behavior.

Waiting for Mikki to return, Rory sat alone, gnawing her lip as she watched yet another couple match up. The lucky pair proceeded to the stage where Maureen Baxter handed them a prize and dropped their ticket into the wire bin containing all the entries for the evening.

The impending raffle for the grand prize of a weekend at Painter's Cove resort in Mendocino was the unofficial wrap-up to the evening. Surely then Rory would be able to leave. Lauren had already disappeared, after being spotted early on with a smoldering Johnny Depp look-alike. Some sisters had all the luck.

A sloppy drunk in a Niners jersey staggered off the dance floor with the bottle of beer that had obviously been his only constant companion for the evening. He waggled his key at Rory.

"Why not?" she said with a sigh, and held out her necklace.

The guy aimed his key at the tiny lock on the suitcase and missed by a mile, thrusting the miniature key into her cleavage instead. He emitted a high-pitched giggle. "Missed my mark."

"Let me." She pried the key from his sticky fingers and inserted it into the lock. No go.

She returned the key with a relieved smile. *Thanks for small favors.*

However, her "possibilities" were rapidly dwindling. She scanned the room again, telling herself that she was looking for Mikki, not Tucker. She'd spotted him frequently in the past hour, seemingly trying his key on every girl who caught his eye.

Had he found his match yet?

Not that she cared. Life was too short to waste on men who ran hot and cold—hot when they were one-on-one and their sap was running, cold when their friends showed up and suddenly they didn't want to be seen with the "fat girl."

Lauren would gasp and say, "But you're not fat!"

Mikki would say, "Screw 'em if they don't appreciate you."

Her mother, Emma Constable, would not even understand the issue. Rory had inherited her height and shape from Emma, who carried herself with the grace of a queen and had not a shred of self-consciousness about being *zaftig*. As mortifying as Rory had found her mother during adolescence—a time already made bad enough by dint of a body that was six inches and thirty pounds bigger than most of the other girls—she'd learned to live with Emma's openness about all things sexual.

The woman collected male admirers with an ease that was astounding. Even inspiring. Rory's foster sisters had called it Emma's mojo. There could be no better proof that sexual attraction wasn't only about bodies, but brains, as well.

Unfortunately, Rory's brain still got more action than her body. Even so, she was hopeful. Always hopeful.

But not desperate.

She undid the catch on her necklace and slipped off the damned thing. The prizes didn't matter to her. What hurt was that she'd let herself believe, for a short while, that she might meet someone who'd not only see the inner her, but be equally enticed by the outer person.

She knew she wasn't unattractive. There'd been a handful of admirers over the years. But she'd never be a Barbie doll with a twenty-two-inch waist, and that narrowed her options a lot.

Suddenly her pulse leaped. There was Tucker, near the bar. No key partner yet.

He was in a conversation with a man Rory had noticed throughout the evening, moving from woman to woman with his key out. The slavering hound-dog type.

The man gestured. Tucker talked fast, looking right at her for a couple of seconds before deliberately turning away. Her face flushed with heat as they surreptitiously exchanged keys.

"Ready to go?" Mikki plopped onto a stool and put her chin on her hand. Her eyelids lowered sleepily. "What're you looking at?"

"Nothing," Rory said. There was no reason for her to believe that Tucker had palmed off his key—the key that he'd avoided fitting into her locket—on the other guy.

No reason except her own self-doubt.

She grabbed the evening bag that matched her boutique version of an ethnic batik dress. "Let's go."

"Wait." Mikki pushed back her tousled hair. "Did you find your key partner yet?"

"Nope, and I'm giving up. I'll drop the necklace off at the door in case someone else wants to try it."

"What about the prizes? The movie tickets?"

Rory was an avowed film buff, but not even tickets to a red carpet premiere would entice her to stick around. "I've had enough humiliation, thanks, Mikki. I'm leaving. Unless you'd rather get a ride home from Nolan, I suggest you come with me."

"Nolan. That son of a—" Mikki sputtered peppery insults as she climbed off the stool, looking a bit wobbly. She'd definitely been drinking more than diet cola.

Rory took a firm grip on her sister's arm. "I'm not letting you get away this time. Are you ready to tell me what happened between you and Nolan?"

"Make that what *didn't* happen." Mikki extricated her heel from the rungs of the stool and pulled herself upright. Her blue eyes sharpened through the haze of alcohol. "Namely, our divorce."

"What!"

"The rat bastard told me the divorce was never legal. Right before he smiled and stuck his key in my lock." Mikki was clearly outraged by the encounter. "*Then* he went and walked out on me before we collected our prize! But never mind." She patted her purse. "I'll be much happier at the B and B in Napa without him."

Rory's mind was pedaling to catch up to speed. "You and Nolan are still married?"

"Technically." Mikki let out another colorful oath. "But not for long. I'll take care of that damn fast, lemme tell ya."

"Before you rush into anything, it wouldn't hurt to take some time to think the situation through." Rory had always believed that despite Mikki's injured pride, there remained a strong connection between her and Nolan, her first true love. Maybe even her one and only.

But her sister wasn't in any mood to listen to reason. "Hey, Tuck, old friend!" Mikki waved. "Come say bye-bye."

He lifted a hand in acknowledgment and headed their way.

Rory rolled her eyes. Super. Maybe *now* he'd try his key on her, but the joke would be on him because the guy he'd exchanged with hadn't approached her, either. Tuck's odds were still the same.

"No match?" Mikki said as she leaned in to kiss Tucker's cheek.

He gave her back a pat. "I guess it's not my night."

A sly smile appeared on Mikki's face. "Rory's still unattached."

Rory put on a cease-and-desist look, but Mikki didn't stop. Apparently she was getting payback for her big sis refusing to hand over the car keys when she'd wanted to run from Nolan.

"Go ahead and try her," Mikki cooed. "You two might be a perfect fit."

Tucker looked at Rory and raised his brows. She nodded grimly. There was no avoiding it.

"Stranger things have happened," she said through gritted teeth. She lifted the necklace off the table, pinching the chain between two fingers. She held it high, at arm's length.

Her eyes speared Tucker. "Dare you."

"I'd be happy to." With a blameless innocence that was as fake as a nugget of fool's gold in Rory's estimation, he caught the dangling charm in his fingers and took the key from his pocket. It slid into the lock and turned with a *snick,* springing the miniature suitcase open. He pulled out the slip of paper printed with their number—178—and a section to fill out with their contact information for the raffle.

Rory stared at Tucker. He didn't seem surprised. Nor disappointed. What an actor.

Mikki applauded drunkenly. "I knew you two were a match." She gestured at her sister's shawl and the similar hue of his shirt. "You see? Color-coordinated. It must be destiny."

Rory forced a smile. "Since when do you believe in destiny?" Mikki wouldn't trust her future to something as flimsy as destiny; she believed in fighting tooth and nail for what was right.

"I don't." Mikki's nose crinkled. "But you do."

Rory snorted, though she couldn't argue very strenuously. She'd been raised with Emma's belief system, which incorporated homespun common sense with the wisdom of the Dalai Lama, the teachings of the Eternal Sunshine Church of Peace, Love and Understanding, the Bible, runes, Tarot cards and even the occasional visit from a Jehovah's Witness who'd knock on the door at Garrison Street and soon find him or herself with an invitation for supper.

"You two work this out and I'll go up and get our prize," offered Tucker.

As soon as he was gone Rory said, "I'm going to kill you," to her sister.

Mikki had no fear. "How come? Tuck's a wonderful guy."

"He didn't want to try his key on my lock."

"Could have fooled me."

"Trust me. I'm not his type." Or so he wanted to think.

Mikki focused with one eye, her head wavering. "And you know this how?"

"He doesn't even remember me," Rory admitted. She dropped the necklace, Tucker's key still inserted, into her bag. "We met once, when Lauren and I threw that party for you and Nolan after your elopement. Tucker looked right at me tonight without so much as a soupçon of recognition."

"You've changed a lot, Rory. And my marriage happened years ago." Mikki's one open eye clouded. "Ancient history. I barely remember those days myself."

"You are such a liar. You've never resolved your feelings for Nolan, but at last you two have a second chance to work out the marriage."

"Second chances are for wishy-washy women. That's so not me."

"You know what Mom would say, don't you?"

They looked at each other and repeated, "'The wheel never stops turning. What goes around, comes around.'"

Mikki scoffed. "That and a chorus of 'Hakuna Matata' might buy me a cappuccino at Starbucks."

Although a lot of the crowd had cleared out of Clementine's, the remaining guests were gathering around the stage where Maureen was about to announce the raffle winners. Rory and Mikki joined the applause as she read off an approximate total of the money they'd raised tonight for the building fund. An impressive amount. The transitional house for troubled girls in crisis, already under construction, was ensured a good foundation.

"We've done our duty for Baxter House." Rory grabbed Mikki's arm. "Let's get out of here before Tucker comes back."

"This is why you don't have a lover," Mikki protested as she was towed away. "You back up and turn around at the first bump in the road."

"As opposed to you, the Pint-Size Steamroller," Rory said. "We all have our ways."

Tucker's voice stopped them. "Where are you going?"

"Home," Rory said, not stopping.

"The ladies'," Mikki said, stopping. With a wriggle, she tugged the hem of her mini over her thighs. "You keep an eye on Rory for me."

Reluctantly, Rory stopped and turned toward Tucker, clasping her shawl and purse against her abdomen. Despite the big fans whirring up near the vaulted ceiling, the club was quite hot. Damp strands of hair clung to her neck and cheeks. Her makeup had probably melted long ago.

"I put our number into the raffle." Tucker held out two tickets. "And we won a couple of movie passes."

"Super." She peeled away one ticket. "We won't even have to sit together."

His brows pulled down into a frown and for an instant she was hit with a wallop right beneath her rib cage. Regret…longing. Sharp enough to steal her breath.

Was she so afraid of being rejected that she wouldn't even take a chance?

"Or we can go as friends," she amended. Safe territory.

The tightness in Tucker's jaw relaxed. "That's better."

Of course. He was a nice guy, Nolan's buddy. He didn't want to hurt her feelings, so he was determined to do the friends thing. She could be a good sport and go along with it, no problem. They could *both* pretend that he hadn't snacked on her neck and squeezed her ass under the guise of dancing, then changed his mind when the fog had cleared.

She could also pretend that she didn't know about his attempt to avoid her with the switched keys.

"Entry to the grand prize raffle is officially closed," Maureen announced from the stage. She pointed into the crowd. "You, gorgeous. How about coming up here to spin me 'round?"

A blond beach god vaulted up to the stage and gave Maureen a twirl before proceeding over to the barrel holding the numbered tickets. "Oo-oh," Maureen said into the microphone, fanning her face. "Suddenly I'm so dizzy."

The bantering continued while the hunk cranked the handle. The mesh drum whirled. Rory craned her neck toward the swagged alcove that opened to the bathrooms. Mikki wouldn't slip away, would she, out of a misguided attempt to throw Rory and Tucker together?

He'd put his hand between her shoulder blades and nudged her toward the crowd.

"The grand prize tonight is an all-inclusive, three-day weekend at Painter's Cove in Mendocino. Our lucky couple will stay in one of their luxury suites—"

Several in the crowd tittered. Maureen wagged a finger and put her mouth up against the microphone, dropping her voice to a husky intimate tone. "Sleeping arrangements to be determined by private consultation." She went on to list amenities such as private pool and spa, plus a number of gratis appointments for massages and facials and a tee time at the golf course. Finally she signaled for a drumroll before reaching into the basket.

To a cheer and the crash of a cymbal, Maureen waved the chosen bright pink ticket overhead. Her chiffon sleeves fluttered. "And our winner is—" she unfolded the paper "—number one hundred seventy-eight!"

Rory was poking through her purse, looking for Mikki's keys.

Tucker gripped her elbow. "That's us. One seventy-eight."

"Oh, no. I'm sure you're mistaken. We're one eighty-seven…"

"Tucker Schulz," Maureen read off the ticket. "And Rory Constable! Woohoo, Rory!" She put a hand over her eyes and searched the crowd. "Is that you, honey? Come on up and get your prize."

Suddenly, Mikki was pushing Rory toward the stage and Tucker had her hand, helping her up the steps. She felt herself flushing, going awkward and tongue-tied, the way she often did when she was the center of attention. Her desire to be more self-assured was not always matched by the execution.

"Rory is the owner of San Francisco's own Lavender Field, the chain of bakeries that supplied the desserts that those of you not on low-carb diets have been enjoying tonight." Maureen's boisterous laugh rang out. She gave Rory a hug before returning to the mike. "And Tuck is an electrician who's promised to wire Baxter House free of charge. Let's give our lucky couple a hand, folks. We couldn't have selected a more deserving pair."

Tucker said "Thanks" into the microphone.

Rory plastered a smile on her face, then gave a little wave at Mikki, who was swinging a fist in the air, hooting and hollering.

Maureen took over again and thanked everyone for their support for the cause so dear to her heart.

Gratefully out of the spotlight, Rory faded away to the side of the stage. "I can't believe we won. And you didn't even want to—" The words choked off.

Tucker stood directly in front of her, his fingertips resting on her bare arms, burning holes in her concentration. "Didn't want to…?"

"Be my key partner," she blurted.

"What makes you say that?"

"I saw you exchange keys with some drunken guy. Before, near the bar."

An expression that looked a lot like guilt bled into Tucker's face. "I wasn't avoiding you, Rory. The guy approached me. I didn't know him from Adam, but he'd had no luck with his key and he, uh, I guess his eye was on a certain woman…"

"And your key fit her lock? That makes no sense."

Tucker hesitated. "My original key may not have, but he knew his didn't. He'd tried his key on her. And everyone else."

"Except me." Rory tipped her chin up. The hell if she'd let him see her humiliation at being considered the very least desirable woman in Clementine's. This was worse than being picked last for dodgeball in gym class, but at least it hadn't been Tucker who'd avoided her then. Tucker, a man she still found extremely attractive, despite her attempts not to.

She continued blindly. "He persuaded you to take me—my locket, I mean."

"Didn't take much persuading." Tucker's eyes gleamed. "I was perfectly willing to exchange."

"Oh." She blinked, realizing the full implications. Tucker had switched keys knowing that he was likely to be her match.

Out of the goodness of his heart, she reminded herself, should her libido decide to reengage over the gentlemanly gesture. *Because they were friends.*

He ducked his chin to peer into her eyes. "Okay?" His voice was soft, warm. Kind. Not his fault that her heartbeat ratcheted up several notches every time he looked at her.

"Okay," she said, giving him a quick nod.

He grinned. "You're my lucky number. We'll have a great time in Mendocino."

Rory held her tongue. She could deal with being his friend if she had to, but doing so while undergoing three days of body-baring sun and fun?

That was asking too much of her.

Or not enough—if he was serious about the hands-off policy.

3

A BLAST OF COLD water hit Tucker's shins, streaming all over his flip-flops. "Hey!" He stepped out of the spray, removed his wet sandals and shook them off on the plot of grass that was the lawn. "What was that for?"

"I'm waking you up," said Sam, the hose-wielder and Tuck's eldest brother. "No one turns down a free weekend in Mendocino."

It was late Sunday afternoon in the narrow backyard of his parents' venerable Victorian row house, where the day's allotment of sunshine was slowly being diffused by an incoming fog. They'd taken the kids beachcombing after church.

Upon the clan's return home in their fleet of vehicles, the women had immediately gone inside to work on dinner while banishing the men outdoors with orders to hose off the munchkins. Tuck's nieces and nephews had brought half of the beach with them in their sandy skin, clothes and hair. The other half was on the floor mats of his pickup.

"Free carries a high price when there are too many strings attached," he said, sorry that he'd brought up the events at the key party. But his siblings had already known that he'd gone and there had been no way Didi would let him get away without offering up a full report.

"What strings?" Sam said. "You're so stringless you don't even wear sneakers."

Tuck lobbed one of the flip-flops at his brother, who caught the sandal with a squidging noise and immediately tossed it to the family dog, Chuckie Doll. The Golden Retriever sank his teeth into the rubber sole and ran off to have himself a good chew, feathered tail wagging.

"Thanks a lot, you bastard."

Sam was unconcerned. "Punishment for lying."

"Who's lying?"

"You know you want to go."

Tuck raked a hand through his hair, trying to line up his pinball reactions to Rory. He should have called game over, but he kept bouncing around instead, rebounding between reasons for and against seeing her again. "Let's put it this way. Have you ever known a woman to go away for the weekend and *not* throw out a few strings?"

"Been known to happen." Sam got a fond look on his face. For all that he looked like a suburban forty-something dad in khakis with graying hair, in his early twenties Sam had been a bachelor about town. Women had got hot at the sight of him in his fire-fighting gear. A few of the conquests from his past had even accused him of being a player, a point Sam's wife brought up with glee whenever she was in a snarky mood.

"Not with this woman." Tuck shook his head. Rory was the marriage-minded type. Although the memory of their dance made his sunburned toes curl into the cool grass, so did the look in her eye when the subject of babies had been brought up. There might come a day when he was ready for that, but not yet.

Sam remained skeptical. "You met her at a *key* party, for chrissake. I never thought I'd see the day you turned into a hipster."

"I had to go." Tuck thanked his lucky stars Sam hadn't seen him in the silk shirt. "Blame Nolan. He's sniffing after Mikki again."

Sam nodded. Nolan had grown up with the Schulzes, almost one of the family. He'd seemed to be at their house more often than his own. They'd all kicked back and enjoyed a few beers this past weekend.

"The boy has it bad," Sam said. "Which can feel pretty good with the right woman. You'll find out what I mean when you meet her, same way I did."

Tuck grinned. "I like it just as well with the wrong woman."

"Ah, so the mystery lady is *that* kind."

"Nope." Tuck circled a finger in the air. "Do a one-eighty. Think of her more like one of Didi's best friends than a fast-and-loose club girl."

Their oldest sister had a network of female friends who were smart, outspoken and determined to have it all. Individually, they were manageable. As a group, they scared the stuffing out of Tucker and his brothers. Especially the single ones. Whenever they came near, he felt the marriage manacles locking around his wrists.

"Yeesh. Rotten luck for you since you're stuck with her." Sam squirted the hose at the kids. They ran in circles chasing after his oldest boy, who held a soccer ball out of the younger kid's reach.

"Rotten luck?" Tucker brushed down his T-shirt and ragged denim shorts. "I wouldn't say that, either."

Sam's knowing laugh rumbled beneath the shrieks of the children. After all, he'd married one of Didi's friends. "Tell me about this chick. Whatever she's got, you obviously want."

"Nah. All she's got is our room reservation for Painter's Cove."

"What's her name?" Gabe chimed in, walking over from where he'd been playing with his toddler in a bouncy swing. He was the second brother, an ex-minor leaguer turned college baseball coach, father of two, married to a Southern redhead named Lula.

Tuck opened then closed his mouth. "Not telling. You'll spill the beans to your wife and next thing I know, the whole crew of them will be slow-cooking me into a relationship."

"True." Gabe laughed from the perch he'd taken on top of their parents' ancient cedar picnic table. "Lula has her ways of getting me to talk."

"So does Karen," Sam said. "But her ways involve a meat fork planted in my skull."

Tuck chuckled. The banter was a familiar refrain. In reality, he saw how devoted his brothers were to their families, day in, day out. And he admired that—from a distance. "You're encouraging me to settle down because…?"

"My wife makes me," Sam said.

They laughed.

"What's the big deal, anyway?" Gabe asked. "Take the vacation. You don't have to marry the girl because you've shared a room."

"Right," Tucker said, unconvinced.

Logically he should have had no hesitation since Rory wasn't his type. Okay, so she was a little less not his type than he'd first thought, but still…

"I'll be sure she understands we're going as friends," he told his brothers.

Sam's forehead wrinkled. "Yeah, that'll work."

"Do I detect a note of skepticism?"

"Proceed with a healthy caution, my pal. Watch your step around her and you'll be fine."

"It's his hands he's got to watch," Gabe put in.

Sam grinned. "Tuck was always good with his hands."

"On the job. Strictly on the job," Tucker protested, knowing it was no use even though he had calluses on his fingertips from wrapping wire, not squeezing female behinds.

"Yeah, sure." Gabe looked at Sam. "Remember the time we caught him with his hands up Mary-Anne Shanahan's shirt on the living room couch? He looked like he was calibrating the engine of a Maserati."

"And when we threw on the lights—"

"He jumped up—"

"With a boner capable of parting the Red Sea."

"And he said—"

"'I was only measuring her for a T-shirt.'"

"And Mary-Anne said…"

Sam and Gabe synchronized for the big finish, "'They're 34C.'"

"Shut it," Tuck commanded through their booming laughter, even though he had no real hope of quelling them. As the youngest of five, he'd been the subject of their merciless teasing all his life. He'd learned to roll with it by keeping a sense of humor and always being alert for revenge opportunities. Like the surprise male strip-o-gram he'd arranged for Gabe and Lula's honeymoon.

Didi came into the backyard, banging the screen door behind her. "Quit torturing my baby brother," she said, and began issuing orders like a drill sergeant. Sam's trigger finger twitched on the hose nozzle, but one narrow look from Didi and he ambled off, compliantly reeling up the hose.

Gabe was dispatched to round up the hooligans. "Fried chicken," he yelled across the yard. "First one at the dining table gets a drumstick."

Tuck took cover from the rush, ducking to sit at the picnic table.

Didi plopped beside him. "How many brothers does it take to screw in a lightbulb?"

"More than three?" he guessed.

"Nope. No one knows how many, because they're too busy screwing with each other's heads."

Tuck moaned. "Like you don't want to do the same."

"Of course I don't." Didi draped an arm around his shoulders. "I'm only interested in your future happiness."

"I'm doing just fine in the present, thanks." And he was. He'd dropped out of college with the idea that he'd try pro surfing, but had wound up making a living in the construction trade instead. After going through a period of feeling his oats and drifting from job to job, he'd been working steadily as a licensed electrician for seven years now. Recently he'd bought into the four-plex with Didi and Sam, even agreeing to serve as the on-site landlord and handyman. How much more settling did she want out of him?

As if he had to ask.

"You're doing it again." He made a motion to grab her by the head.

She jerked away and dusted mussed hair off her face. "What? I haven't even begun." The last time they'd had this conversation she'd conceded that her bossiness was annoying and had promised that all he had to do was to put her into one of the Schulz brothers' dreaded headlocks to remind her to shut the hell up.

"I saw the look in your eye," he said. "You were going to mention Charla again."

"I'm looking at the Andersons' yard. Their phlox is blooming." Didi could never pull off the innocent act. She was too sharp to play dumb.

"And I think your nose is growing." The boys had always teased her that, unlike Pinocchio, her nose didn't grow with a lie, but only when she was about to stick it up in somebody's business.

She touched it. Snub, with freckles, the only feature about her that wasn't strong, square or firm. "All right.

I won't tell you what you should do. But in my version of your life—"

He coughed a "Bossy wench" under his breath.

She went on, always good at talking over resistance. "You should still be dating Charla, not a barfly from Clementine's. You'll never find anyone good at one of those clubs."

"Ah, but you didn't get to see the miniskirts and butt cleavage tattoos."

"I didn't say good-looking. I said good. You need a *good* woman, Tuck. Like Charla." Charla was one of Didi's girlfriends, a high-powered executive who'd finally broken the snooze alarm on her biological clock. She was on a five-year plan to gain a husband and child.

"Look, Deeds. When we went out, Charla made it clear that a mere electrician wasn't good enough for her. She wanted me to become a contractor and builder, then a developer—the kind with an expensive office suite and a hard hat for show only. I don't want to date a woman who has ambitions for me."

"I know Charla can be pushy, but I thought you two might be a good match. She needs a little lightheartedness and you need the discipline."

"Are we talking S and M here?"

"Quit kidding around, Tuck." Didi frowned. "What's wrong with a little ambition?"

Tucker couldn't think up a flip response. "Nothing. When I'm ready for it, I'll get my own."

"Lazy boy," she chided. "You always did get away with murder, skipping chores to go surfing and the like. Comes with being the youngest, I suppose."

He raised his brows. "Or a bad reaction to always being told what to do my brothers and sisters."

She smiled. "You have a point. If I tell Charla to knock off the pressure, would you consider—"

"Sorry. The chemistry wasn't there."

"How can you be sure? Chemistry doesn't always combust at first sight."

"No." Tucker thought of meeting Rory. He'd looked right past her. Big mistake, though he'd corrected it before too long. "But I dated Charla twice and have run into her a dozen times over the past months because she's always at your house when I come by—"

He broke off to shoot a glare at his sister, who didn't have the grace to look guilty. Didi didn't do guilt. Not on herself, anyway. "I won't be asking her out again, Deeds. Not ever. So give it up or prepare to be headlocked."

"All right. I know when I'm beat." She sighed. "Tell me about this Miss Clementine who's got her claws in you. French-manicured claws, I'll bet. And she wears Manolos and carries a supply of handy condoms in her itty-bitty purse."

He laughed. "You're getting prudish in your old age."

Didi looked horrified at the suggestion. "Then please tell me I'm wrong."

"You're wrong. She's not what you think."

"Yeah, she has *depth*." Didi rolled her eyes.

"Do you remember the first time Max picked you up? He drove up on a motorcycle, tattoos on both arms, his hair in a ponytail and a sneer beneath his Fu

Manchu. Not the optimal date for a seventeen-year-old, but Mom and Dad let you do your own thing."

"They did not! They banned me from seeing him again. I had to sneak out the window until I turned eighteen."

"Okay, but you get my point. Look at Max now." A balding orthodontist whose kids colored in his tattoos with Magic Markers, he and Didi had been married for almost twenty years. Their eldest son would be entering college this coming fall.

Didi glowered. "I hate when you make a rational argument against me."

"See how I've matured," Tucker teased, though he hoped she'd recognize the truth in his words. While it was true that he'd coasted through life up to now, he wasn't averse to a change in speed—or even direction. He'd always figured that one day he'd come across a woman worth stopping for, and then he'd know what all the hoopla over love was about.

Their mother cranked open the kitchen window and yelled for them to get their butts inside before dinner got cold. Just like old times, when they'd all lived at home and been the scourge of the neighborhood.

"You could have simply told me to leave you alone," Didi said as they walked to the back door.

Tuck gave the top of her head an affectionate kiss. "Has that ever worked?"

"No better than a headlock," she said sassily, sliding out from under his arm when he tried to tighten his grip. She hurtled herself inside, banging the screen door shut on Tucker's nose.

THE SCENT of smoked jasmine lingered in the air at Emma Constable's house hours after the brunch was over. Surrounded by a pile of pillows and cushions in the bay-window seat, Rory was so at ease she hadn't moved for more than an hour. She'd even drifted off for a while after the talking had ended and Lauren and Mikki had gone home. Now Emma had come in from the garden and was gliding back and forth in the kitchen, rattling ice trays and running water, humming "Light My Fire" to herself.

Rory gave a long stretch and yawn. Herbal tea, fresh bread, incense—those were the smells of her mother's house. And often her own.

Like mother, like daughter? The similarities were both comforting and aggravating. If only she'd been able to consciously choose which traits she'd inherit.

"Sangria, hon?" Emma asked, drifting in from the kitchen with a tall glass filled with ice cubes and a pale pink liquid. She'd changed from the sparkly caftan she'd worn earlier into a T-shirt and a pair of faded jeans. Her feet were bare, the nails painted bright red. "I can make sandwiches—bean sprouts and hummus."

"No thanks." Rory straightened the pillows, using one to smother a second yawn. "I should probably be going. What time is it?"

"Five-ish."

"Whew. I had a longer nap than I thought."

Emma's eyes narrowed. "Are you feeling all right? Take some of my ginseng. It'll put zip in your step."

"I'm fine. Been catching up on sleep from the other

night at Clementine's. I was up early the past two mornings—"

"You work too hard."

"It wasn't work." Just restlessness. Rory found it tough to break the habit of waking before dawn to bake her daily bread, as she'd done for years while getting her first stores launched. Now that she had store managers and most of the baking was done in an industrial kitchen outside of the city, she left the early morning hours to others. Yet the early-to-bed habit remained.

Yawning at 9:00 p.m. tended to cut into her appeal as a swinging single.

"Then what, hon? You were reticent at brunch." Emma set her drink on a side table.

"What do you mean? We talked for *hours*."

"Hashing out Lauren's flash-dating intrigues and Mikki's Nolan Baylor complication." With a soulful moan—Emma did everything with soul—she sank into an artisan-made rocking chair, flung one leg over the arm, wiggled her butt into the cushion, then pushed off with the ball of her foot. "You said nothing about yourself. If Lauren hadn't mentioned that you'd won the grand prize…"

Rory shrugged.

Her mother's brow furrowed as she took up a bundle of hand-carded wool. The click of knitting needles made a counterpoint to the rhythmic creak of the old rocking chair. Rory felt along the floor for the shoes she'd kicked off, but she was in no rush to leave. The familiar smells and sounds of her mother's house were soothing to the battered soul. She, Mikki and Lauren certainly didn't return for the bitter tea.

"The house is so quiet," Rory said.

"Arun is working." Emma's remaining boarder, a foster child who'd come of age, was looking for an apartment of his own. "And Ernie spends most of his time in his room, meditating." Ernesto Modesta, a compatriot from Emma's commune days, had arrived at her door the past month, asking for a bed. He was supposed to move on anyday now. No one was holding their breath. "But you're avoiding the subject, m'dear."

"Only because I have nothing to tell."

Emma smiled. "Do you think I've lost my touch?" She tapped one of the needles to her nearly unlined forehead. "I may need bifocals now, but my third eye sees as well as ever, Aurora. The less you say, the more I'm sure there's something big going on in your head. Why don't you talk it out? You always kept your worries too much to yourself."

"Some of us don't feel the need to announce our every body twinge and passing thought to the general public."

Emma was unperturbed. "Bottling up your emotions isn't healthy. When was the last time you had a colonic?"

Gawd! Rory flung herself back against the pillows. She gazed up at the sitting room's antique tin ceiling, original to the house, and counted to ten. "I am *fine*, Mom. Both physically and emotionally. Quit looking for trouble."

Her mother shrugged. *Creak, creak. Click, clack.*

Blessed peace. Rory was almost lulled.

Emma speared a loop of yarn. "No decision yet on the baby question?"

Oh, damn. *That.* Baby-making had not been on Rory's mind the past few days, except in a recreational capacity. "I only said I was *considering* having a baby. You know, mulling it over. I'm not anywhere close to a decision."

"My friends Deena and Azure went to a sperm bank."

Rory made a face. "Jerry Garcia being no longer available."

"Jerry was always a generous man," Emma said fondly before returning to Rory's dilemma. "All I'm saying is, keep your options open."

"I'm not so hard up that I can't find a donor on my own." Though Rory had her doubts. Her baby daydreams had gone as far as wondering who would be the father, but hadn't gotten much beyond that even though there were several good male friends she could ask. Too large a part of her still wanted to go the traditional marriage route.

Which was odd, given her upbringing. Her father, one of Emma's many lovers, had drifted into Rory's life at infrequent intervals, acting more like a friendly, but distant, uncle than a dad. Larger-than-life Emma had filled in for the lack with supreme confidence. She'd been everything—father, mother, disciplinarian, instigator, best friend.

Rory worried a ragged cuticle. On second thought, perhaps her inclination to experience the one type of family life Emma couldn't provide was not so odd. She had immense respect for her mother, but not everyone could live up to her example.

"A grandchild would be nice." Emma rocked, placid and obdurate. Every child who arrived at Garrison Street soon learned that for all of Emma's go-with-the-flow philosophies, she was also the original immovable object. "You don't need to approach this like a business decision, sweetie. A baby is Mother Nature at her finest. Plant a seed, it will sprout. The practical details will work out."

Rory squirmed. She'd change the subject, but the only other one that sprang to mind was sex. Her sisters were comfortable discussing the details of their sex lives with Emma. Rory less so. "I can't believe you're trying to talk me into having a baby on my own. Whatever happened to family values?"

"Don't try to distract me with political posturing. I wouldn't be going along with the idea if I wasn't sure it's something you truly want." Emma rearranged her tangled skein of yarn. "Lauren and Mikki and I will always be here to help. It takes a village…"

"I know, but that's not the point."

"Don't tell me you want a husband first."

Rory pressed her knuckles against her smile. "I know it's a radical idea, but you raised me to be an independent thinker."

Her mother sniffed. "I have nothing against the concept of life mates."

"And marriage vows…?"

Brows raised, Emma peered at Rory over the rim of her reading glasses. "If you must."

"Don't worry. I have no prospects at the moment, for either a husband or a father."

"What about the young man you're going to Mendocino with?"

"I haven't decided about that."

"Hmm. I've forgotten his name."

"I didn't tell you."

"One of the girls must have mentioned him during brunch."

There was no hiding. "Tucker Schulz." Rory's stomach flipped over. "Don't get any ideas. His only potential is as a friend."

Emma's all-knowing gaze was on Rory's face; she felt it heating up. "Mikki knows him?"

"He's Nolan's best friend."

"Interesting."

"No, it's not. Not for my part." But her mother had always been able to read her like a book and it was clear she could see past Rory's avowals even when she continued to deny her interest.

After a moment the knitting needles resumed clicking. "There's nothing wrong with going as friends."

Nothing right about it, either, Rory thought. She'd be asking for trouble. So far, Mikki was still talking about researching divorce laws and filing new papers to end her marriage, but they'd been close for too long. Rory knew how much feeling her sister had buried under the hard-hearted act.

Which meant Tucker was right. If they had a weekend fling, and then Nolan and Mikki ended up together after all, they'd be forced to see each other over and over, in the most awkward of social circumstances. Some women were able to keep ex-lovers as friends— namely her mother. Rory doubted she could be as equable. For years after Brad had dumped her, she'd avoided his neighborhood and their mutual friends. When he'd moved away, her relief had been enormous.

But this was Tucker, not Brad. Was she so afraid of the possible consequences that she'd give up the grand prize trip? There was caution, and then there was stupidity.

Rory couldn't remember the last time a man had taken her to such a high level of attraction so quickly. Judging by Tucker's actions—and reactions—he shared at least some of her fascination.

Any future awkwardness might be worth it, she told herself. Their explosive chemistry indicated a risk worth taking.

4

ALMOST TWO WEEKS LATER Rory was called to the phone at her Chestnut Street bakery in the Marina, where she spent most of her time. There were rare days when she could sit back and let her store managers do the work while she congratulated herself on the efficiency of her operation. Then there were times when seemingly a million small problems cropped up and she was at the center of most of them.

This was one of those days. She'd been on the phone or on her feet all day.

"Take a message," she said to the employee who held the kitchen phone in one hand and a big spoon covered with slime in the other.

"I tried, but she said it's Maureen Baxter."

Rory inched out from below the mammoth industrial sink. "This is hopelessly clogged. We have to call a plumber. Katya, can you take care of that?" The drain had spewed smelly sludge when she'd managed to get the pipe open. Her first and favorite unclogging method of jabbing a wooden spoon into the works hadn't worked.

"I'm on it." Katya, the store manager, tossed the spoon into the trash, then handed Rory a white towel.

She wiped her hands before taking the phone. "Yes, Maureen?"

"Rory, my darling Clementine. I simply had to call to say thank you one more time for your generosity. I just returned from the Baxter House location and the work they've accomplished in the time since our fundraiser is incredible."

"I'm glad to hear it, but you really must stop thanking me, Mo. I was happy to help in my small way." Not only had Rory donated the bread and bakeries for the event at Clementine's, but she'd been so inspired by Maureen that she'd mailed off a large check this past week.

"You should stop by the site. It's quite something. Apparently we were mentioned in the blog of some obscure online magazine, and now the volunteers are crawling out of the woodwork. Everyone from Barry Bonds to the mayor has lent a hand, and you know what a coup it is to get Barry."

"Wonderful. I guess the blog wasn't that obscure after all." Although she was secretly pleased to hear that Lauren's *Inside Out* blog had such a faithful following, Rory was only half listening. Despite the exhaust fan, the air in the kitchen was ripe with the stink from the burping sink. She pointed and flapped the towel, motioning for Katya to prop open the back door.

"My current task is to see that the construction proceeds without delay," said Maureen.

"Good luck." From what Rory had experienced with the ongoing renovation of her newest store, construction *never* proceeded without delay.

"I've been rounding up daily lunchtime donations from local restaurants," Maureen went on. "We can't have our volunteers going hungry."

Aha. "I'd be happy to help," Rory said before Maureen had to ask. "My Castro store is closest to your site. I'll give the manager a call to see what we can set up."

"Thanks scads, Rory. If I get fixings from one of the area delicatessens and bread from you, Baxter House will have the happiest workers on record. Especially if you throw in some of those luscious fruit tarts of yours. The spares will do."

There were no spares. "Absolutely. Count me in. I'll be in touch—"

"Wait!"

Rory stifled a sigh. Naturally she couldn't get away that easily.

"Yes? Is there something else I can help you with, Maureen?" She held the phone between her shoulder and ear while she scrubbed her hands with the disinfectant wipes Katya had passed along.

"I'm also following up on a few leftover details from the party." The timbre of Maureen's voice lost its usual brisk confidence, signaling that she was about to approach a personal area where the outcome was less assured. "I noticed that you haven't arranged a date for your Painter's Cove weekend. Is there a problem with the trip?"

"No, of course not." Rory slowly dried her hands, trying to think up an excuse. "It's a fabulous prize."

Silence on Maureen's end, except for a rapid tapping sound.

Rory imagined her friend's arched brows and puckered lips, her tapping fingernails. Maureen would delve as deep as necessary, which meant that if Rory gave her no satisfaction she'd call Tucker next. The woman had boundary issues.

"Is the problem your key partner?"

"Um…"

"Because I ran into Tucker Schulz at the construction site and aside from looking like quite the dish—" Maureen broke off to make a low humming noise of appreciation. "Oh, sorry. Well-hung tool belts distract me. As I was saying—"

Rory interrupted, not wanting Maureen to say whatever she might say, which with Maureen would likely be something terribly pushy, such as that she'd taken charge and arranged Rory's weekend for her. "There's no problem, Mo. Really. I've been busy, that's all."

"Yes, that's what Tucker claimed."

Oh, yeah? Rory clamped her lower lip between her teeth. She'd made one attempt to reach Tucker and had left a message on his machine.

He hadn't returned the call.

So rude. Since then Rory's stubbornness had kicked in and she was determined to wait for him to make the next move. That he'd be willing to dump an expensive prize to avoid her was not humiliating, not at all.

She'd admit to galling.

"Is there a time limit to use the weekend?" she asked, ready to keep Tucker in a holding pattern for months if she had to. Maybe by then her attraction to him would have fizzled out.

Maureen paused. "I believe you have a year."

"An entire year! Then why is everyone on my case about scheduling this trip immediately?"

"Everyone?" Rory could hear the smile in Maureen's voice. "I may be an important personage, but I hardly qualify as *everyone.*"

"Uh-huh. Everyone, as in my interfering sisters. Was it Mikki or Lauren who set you up to call me on this?"

Maureen laughed, but she didn't answer.

"Mikki, I'll bet." Lauren was less pushy, whereas Mikki had been riding Rory's back like a howler monkey, going on about what a great guy Tucker was and how his connection to Nolan didn't have to put the brakes on his and Rory's relationship.

Sure, Rory thought. It didn't have to. But she'd had enough experience with these things to know that it inevitably did. She might tell herself that she was willing to overlook the potential problems in favor of a shot at great sex, even the short-term version, but reality was another matter. Men got weird about mixing their social and private lives.

"All I'm concerned with is seeing that the prize distribution goes off without a hitch," Maureen said in the prissy voice that intimidated those who didn't know there was a needy child beneath her cool take-charge exterior. "Satisfaction guaranteed."

"Mo, not even you can guarantee satisfaction at a key party."

"But Tucker's a total babe. What's not to like?"

"I like him fine."

"And he likes you."

"Did he say that?" Rory asked, feeling as though she'd been catapulted back to high school.

"I got that impression. Just set a date with him, will you? My reputation is at stake here."

Rory stretched the phone cord to its limit so that she could stand in the short corridor between the kitchen and her office, well away from the employees. Even so, she lowered her voice. "I didn't know you were running an escort service now."

Maureen sniffed. "As if."

"Don't give it another thought, Mo. You're not responsible for matching me and Tucker. You have nothing to do with what happens between us."

Or doesn't happen, she silently added.

"He'd be a perfect Indiana Jones at your next movie-and-dinner party."

Rory smiled. Tucker did have a vintage Harrisonesque manly competence about him. Then there was the Josh Hartnett dimpled grin, halfway between wolfish and boyish…

Maureen's voice came from a distance. "Rory? Do you hear me?"

"Sorry. Well-cocked fedoras distract me." To say nothing of clear green eyes that flickered with a mischievous light and a warm tongue that knew how to find every pulse point in her neck—and probably her entire body.

Mikki and Mo and Lauren and Emma were right. She'd be crazy to pass Tucker up simply out of caution.

"Call him," Maureen urged.

Rory made a sound of assent and that was enough, thank heaven, to get Maureen off the phone.

An idea began brewing. Rory had a brief conversation with Katya about the plumber and the next day's orders. She slipped out of her stained apron and flung it in the laundry hamper, then asked one of the counter girls to box up the day's unsold pastries.

She might not be skilled at seduction, but she knew her other strong suits, and one of them was the surefire way to a man's heart.

FORTUNATELY traffic was slow and Rory didn't have to take her life in her hands to place a few calls on her cell as she worked her way through the city to the Castro store. By the time she'd buzzed through the remaining Lavender Field stock, the back seat of her convertible was piled high with the signature boxes, each one done up with a raffia tie and a sprig of dried lavender affixed with the oval store label.

The cell phone chirped as Rory maneuvered her car into the trickling flow of traffic. She glanced at the display, flicked open the phone and said, "Hello, Lauren."

"Rory—at last! Why haven't you called me? Mikki's been tied up with work all day and I've been dying to hear what happened over the weekend."

"I thought you knew. She did it with him at the B and B."

"Him? Who? *Nolan?*"

"Could there be anyone else?" In a funk over the state of her marriage and a troublesome court case, Mikki had taken off for Napa to enjoy her key party prize in blissful isolation. Nolan had shown up unexpectedly. Or maybe expectedly. Rory hadn't been all that surprised when Mikki had confessed to succumbing to Nolan's seduction. The pair of them had always been hot enough to melt the polar ice caps.

Lauren made a scoffing sound. "Feh. We're talking about Mikki. She might have gone for a revenge bang with the bellhop."

"Nope. Nolan arrived and the two of them went *kaboom*."

"Well, I'm glad she chose screwing him to death over murder."

"There's still that. They've only had sex, not hashed out their problems. Add in her temporary lapse from sobriety and the heart-wrenching case she's working on, and I'm worried." Rory frowned, looking into her rearview mirror as she inched into a lucky parking space very near the Baxter property. A panel truck from a lumberyard had pulled out right in front of her.

"Me, too." Lauren sighed. "We'd better keep an eye on her."

"Hold on to your bra straps, it's going to be a bumpy ride."

"Always is, with Mikki." Lauren must have pulled her phone away. Her voice went faint as she said, "A caramel latte, please."

"You're at the coffeehouse?" Rory asked.

"Just me and my laptop."

"I read 'Lauren's Lies' this morning, the one about swearing off love. Can I assume that you're not happy with Josh since his article about flash-dating you came out?" Lauren's key partner had turned out to be Josh

McCrae, a journalist who'd used the party at Clementine's for article fodder.

"Bingo."

"That's all you have to say?"

"About Josh, yes. But you might be interested to know that I'm researching cybersex for my new assignment. I'll be reporting on the CyberCon for *Left Coast*. It's my shot at the big time."

"Congratulations! I know getting a byline in that magazine has been your goal for ages." And that Lauren had thought her fling with Josh had blown her chances. "But what's CyberCon?"

"Kinky electronic sex. I'll know more after I've seen it firsthand."

"Geesh. You lead this exciting, fascinating life and here I sit with a car full of doughnuts."

"There are days I'd surrender my laptop for one good doughnut," Lauren said. "What are you up to? I hear traffic."

"I'm parked near the Baxter House construction site."

"Oh?"

"My back seat is full of bakery boxes."

"Is this the start to a scene in a construction workers' food fetish video?"

Rory giggled. "Good grief. No, I'm planning to distribute food to the volunteers. There's nothing like a sugar rush after a day of pounding nails in the hot sun."

Lauren went silent for a moment. Rory heard her sip the coffee before she spoke again. "You're hoping Tucker Schulz will be there, aren't you?"

"No." Rory scanned the busy site. Although work had been under way for some time, the structure had only recently taken on the shape of a real building now that the framework was up. "I *know* he's here. Mo told me."

Lauren squeaked. "You're making your move!"

"Not exactly. We'll see how it goes. I may just stuff his mouth with fruit bread and force him to sign the trip over to me."

"Rory, don't be obtuse."

"All right. I'll be nice. I'll be sweet. I'll be his best friend in the world, if that's what he wants."

"Ick."

"Tell me about it. But you never know." Rory slid her sunglasses down, glancing from one worker to another. Sturdy and middle-aged. Young, bald and tattooed. Female. Three guys were shirtless, roasting their glistening muscles in the sun. But none of them was Tucker. "His intentions may change once we're alone."

"Then you think it'll be only a weekend romp?" Lauren sounded worried. She knew that Rory typically invested too much of her heart into her rare affairs to be satisfied with a quickie. Even a spectacular one.

"Maybe. There's a first time for everything. For once, I might be satisfied with a fling."

"Rory. Don't be obtuse," Lauren said again.

"Trust me, I'm going into this with my eyes wide open," she replied, reassuring herself more than her sister. "Talk to you later. I've got to run before the cream puffs melt."

"Call me back right away. I want to know what happens."

"Will do." Rory snapped the phone shut and slid it into her pants' pocket as she climbed out of the car. Lauren would be on the line with Mikki within seconds, relaying the news.

"LOOK AT THAT fine ass," one of the guys said, catching Tucker's attention as he climbed a ladder out of the below-grade maintenance and parking level of the roughed-in structure that would become Baxter House.

Another worker whistled. "Pa-dunk-a-dunk, gimme some junk."

"Show a little respect," Tuck said, until he glimpsed the woman bending over an open convertible door. His mouth went dry. "'Cause she's just been crowned Miss Bootylicious."

While the workers shared a guffaw, Tucker dropped to a narrow strip of dirt and gravel, the only vacant real estate that remained of the expensive city lot. His work boot skidded into a cement block and he almost lost his balance, but his gaze stayed pinned to the visitor.

Hot damn. Fine didn't begin to describe the flagrantly curvaceous form positioned in front of him.

The woman was unloading stacks of white boxes. "Let me help you," he said as the other workers crowded him from behind, also eager to volunteer.

"Thanks." She straightened, turning toward him with her arms filled.

Rory.

"Oh. It's you. I—" She blew at the strands of hair that had fallen into her face. "I didn't see you—that is, I brought treats for the workers." She thrust the bakery boxes into his hands. "Lots of them. Enough for everyone."

"Generous of you."

She smiled distractedly, motioning for the guys to help themselves. In minutes the boxes were whisked away to the construction site, where the volunteers gathered from various areas of the site to pass the goodies around, liberating donuts and rolls and slices of fruit bread by the double handful.

Tucker opened the only remaining box. Beneath a layer of purple waxed paper was a row of glazed doughnuts, puffed to perfection. They looked delicious, but all that he could think of was the similarity they bore to his mental image of Rory's ass in a thong bikini on the beach, oiled up and toasted to a golden brown. The mouth that had gone dry at the first sight of her was now watering.

"You're staring," Rory said. "What's wrong? You don't like doughnuts?"

"Sure I do." He'd better cop to it, as he was about to drool on them. He sucked back his saliva and held the box out to her. "Want one?"

She slid her bottom lip over her teeth. "I shouldn't."

"Carbs?"

"Calories. I'm around bread too much to freak out about a few measly carbs."

His gaze ran down her crisp pantsuit, a taupe herringbone check with the jacket cinched at the waist by a narrow belt of braided leather. Except for the time he'd gone to Armani with Nolan to order a suit, he knew nothing about tailoring. But even a blind man could see that Rory's outfit had been fit to her hourglass curves by a master. She'd managed to appear sleek, classy and ripely sexy all at once.

"You look good." He nodded toward the workers lined up in a row on the retaining wall, watching Rory again now that they'd plowed through the food. "They think so, too. Look at 'em—salivating over you."

She pinkened. "It's the bakery."

"Nah. You make it hard to choose between the two." Tuck turned toward the work site, gesturing at the structure after he'd handed off the doughnuts to the nearest worker. "Do you want the fifty-cent tour?"

"Love it."

"There's not much to see yet." He touched a hand under her elbow as they climbed the backfilled slope, amused by her sharp-toed, narrow-heeled shoes. When she slipped a bit, he put his hand on her backside and give her a small boost.

"Oh!" she squeaked.

One of the workers hopped off the wall and extended a hand. "Allow me."

Rory looked up at the stud—a fraternity member who'd volunteered with his brothers—and nodded. "Thank you."

"Hands off." Tucker shouldered the kid aside. "I'm in charge here."

"Aren't you an electrician, not the foreman?" Rory asked, even though she let him lead her away from the grinning frat boys.

"That's right. I came out today to do some of the preliminary measuring and placement of the breaker box. I won't be doing the actual wiring until later in the process."

She leaned over the foundation wall, bracing her hands on the cement blocks. "Where does that go?"

Tuck tore his eyes away from her outthrust bottom. There was too much testosterone in the air at a construction site. Women visitors should only wear baggy overalls.

He pointed, explaining in broad terms the job he'd be doing. They walked around the perimeter of the foundation wall, studying the bare bones of the framework, the trusses and beams edged in gold by the sinking sun. The volunteers had run out of gas and even the tradesmen were packing up to quit for the day.

"You're very kind, donating your time to the project." Rory looked at him with admiration, her cheeks rosy in the soft light. He felt as if his chest had expanded like a superhero's. "How did you get involved?"

"Nolan. He used to work construction with me, before he went on to law school. I wasn't as ambitious, so I stayed in the trade. When Nolan was bribing Maureen to give him Mikki's key, he threw my skills in to sweeten the deal."

"I thought that might be it."

"Don't get me wrong. I'm happy to help out. I've worked with Habitat for Humanity for years. My entire family does. The Schulzes have a history of charitable work. Unlike the Baylors, we give time instead of money." He shrugged. "Because we have plenty of time, not so much of the latter."

No money? "But you went to school with Nolan, didn't you? I'm sure Mikki mentioned that once."

"Public school. Nolan was kicked out of his ritzy private one."

"Ah. I'd always wondered why you and he—" She broke off. "Don't you live on Telegraph Hill? That's a pricey neighborhood."

"My parents' place. They inherited the house from a spinster aunt. We're blue-collar all the way, so it's been a strain for them to keep up with the maintenance and taxes. One of my sisters and her husband have moved in to help with expenses." Tuck was over-explaining, but something she'd started to say bothered him. And how did she know about his neighborhood?

He cleared his throat. "You wondered what about me and Nolan?"

She gave a small shrug. "Why you became friends."

"Because we're so different, you mean?"

"Yes, I suppose."

"Why do I get the feeling you know more about me than I know about you?"

She cocked her head. "Maybe it's that I remember more."

"Remember?"

"Forget it." She waved a hand, brushing off his curiosity. "What we really need to talk about is this prize we've won."

"Right."

She squinted at him. "You didn't return my call."

"I meant to."

"That's nice and vague."

"Sorry. It's tricky, tiptoeing around our…"

"Our chemistry," she said with more forthrightness than he'd expected.

"Normally, if I go away for the weekend with a woman I'm attracted to, I've got one plan in mind. But this time…well, like I said, it's tricky."

"Don't worry. I have no expectations."

He wasn't sure what she meant. No expectations of sex, or no expectations of a relationship? So he said, "All right."

"Our mutual acquaintances may have other ideas." Her smile was somewhat grim. "Has Nolan been working on you the way my sisters have been working on me?"

"He's been too wrapped up with Mikki and their problems to care who I share a bed with."

"We don't have to share a bed, you know. It's a suite with two beds."

"That's good."

Rory's eyes became flint. "We could probably even go and manage not to see each other at all, if we arrange our schedules carefully enough."

"You know that's not what I meant."

"Of course not." She moved diagonally down the slope, digging her spike heels into the dirt. Pebbles skittered beneath her, but she didn't look for his help. There was a jut to her jaw and a jaunty swing to her hair that he found challenging. Turned out that her warmth was like a woodstove's—banking-hot coals that might flare up at any time.

"I was thinking about *you*," he explained, following. "In case you felt uncomfortable about the situation."

She swung around, forcing him to suddenly pull up. "Why would the prospect of sharing your bed make me uncomfortable?"

How could he answer that without digging himself a deeper hole? For a woman he'd first dismissed as an easygoing earth mother type, he was having a hard time getting a handle on her.

Did she or did she not want to get intimate with him?

"I assumed you're not that kind of woman," he said cautiously.

"*That* kind of woman?" Her eyes rolled. "Then what kind of man would sleeping with me make you?"

He should have stopped right there and pleaded the fifth, especially since he'd lost track of why the conversation had degenerated so quickly. They'd seemed to take a wrong turn as soon as the topic of their chemistry had come up. Usually, for him, chemistry was a natural thing. He rode the skyrocket until it burned out.

Now he was stuck defending himself. "Hey. I know it's a double standard, but I can't help it that men are dogs."

Rory looked at him through narrowed eyes and smiled. Not a comforting smile. "Dogs, hmm? Then it should come as no surprise to you that I'm about to turn into a supreme bitch."

5

RORY WANTED TO POUND her head against the steering wheel. What was wrong with her? She couldn't be a bitch if she tried. When other women were raging with PMS and running their cheating husbands over in a Mercedes, she was making nice or apologizing or making sure that everyone around her was at ease. Growing up in a house full of drama between strong characters, she'd become the peacemaker, the comforter, the mother hen.

But with Tucker, she was…not herself.

He opened the passenger door and climbed in. "I'm sorry."

"No." Her fingers gripped the wheel. "I'm sorry. I don't know what I was saying."

"Yeah, but it was a good line to exit on."

She shot him an assessing look, certain that he was making fun of her. His wry grin seemed hopeful, however. Even conciliatory. He wasn't put off by her tartness.

"Only next time," he added, "you have to leave to be really effective."

"Yeah, well, I'm not good at being a drama queen."

"Thank God. Drama queens harsh my mellow." His smile was relaxing, letting her know he hadn't taken insult.

She breathed deeper. Tucker was the kind of guy who let life's little problems roll off his back. Maybe he could teach her how. "I came here to meet you half-way. I thought we could settle this amicably."

"I didn't know there was anything to settle."

"Splitting the prize."

"That's easy," he said. "We share it, just the way I said we should at the start."

"Isn't that asking for trouble? We don't seem to get along."

"Only when the topic of, uh, our *chemistry* comes up."

"So we should ignore that topic?" Why had she spoken in a question? She knew her own mind.

"As best we can. Unless we decide to go for it."

She shook her head. "I thought you wanted to be friends."

"I'm weak."

Another assessing glance. "I doubt that."

He grinned. "When it comes to females, 'fraid so. I have my mom, two older sisters and four nieces to contend with, in my immediate family alone. They all know how to get their way with me."

"This—" she flicked a finger between them "—is not the same thing."

"Agreed." He shifted in the car seat, rearranging himself so one thigh nearly brushed the gearshift and his arm was draped along the edge of the door.

She smelled eucalyptus, leather, metal, fresh-sawn wood. And a trace of dried perspiration—just enough to make her think of how he'd be, going at it in her bed, naked and sweaty against her lavender-scented sheets, with his tool belt and work boots flung on the fine Persian rug.

She'd worked so hard at giving her life order and beauty, and now she wanted to get dirtied up?

Hell, yeah.

"So we go as friends," she said, fairly certain that wasn't what she wanted out of the weekend, but it was a beginning. If he was truly weak, and if she was willing to accept a dalliance that had no future, they might even have a good time.

"Uh-huh. Friends." From his tone, she suspected that they both knew they were denying the obvious.

She nodded anyway. "Friends. Anything else would be too bothersome."

"Bothersome?"

"Yes. And unwise."

Tucker's brow wrinkled. "I'm glad to know you're such a levelheaded person. I can count on you to keep the weekend—"

Dull, she thought.

"—under control."

"Sure. You'll be like my younger brother," she said with a twinge inside because suddenly she believed she'd figured him out. There were good qualities there—a sense of humor, a gusto for life—but he was also rather contrary and impulsive. He wanted what he couldn't have. If she slapped his hands away, he'd try again. And then it would be all up to her to decide if a temporary boost to her love life would be worth the complications that might ensue.

"That's the smart way to go," Tucker said, even though his face was almost comically screwed into a look of dismay. "Especially with Mikki and Nolan getting back together."

"Are they?"

"If Nolan has his way. I'm betting on my boy."

"We'll see. Mikki may have something to say about that. They're both determined people, and last I heard she hasn't given up on the idea of divorce." On the other hand, Mikki's switch might have been flipped, given her latest report about events at the Napa B and B.

"They run hot and cold." Tucker's hand rubbed up and down his left thigh, calling Rory's eyes to the firm muscle beneath the worn denim.

"I'm glad I'm not so…" Her gaze moved higher to the fullness cupped at his crotch and she lost her train of thought. She moved her mouth, her brain whirred, but she couldn't come up with a single word to say.

"Impulsive?"

She wondered if he was a briefs or boxers guy.

"Impetuous?"

Briefs, going by the shape of things. Definitely briefs. Nice clingy ones.

"Passionate?"

As Tucker's words registered, she shook her head. Impulsive, impetuous, passionate? Exactly what she'd need to be if she wanted to take him on a wild weekend whirl-away.

But also exactly the qualities that she'd once vowed not to let back into her life. Being left at the altar because her groom felt impulsive, impetuous and passionate—for another woman—had killed the appeal of those qualities for her. If that was the extent of what she could expect from Tucker, she'd have to find the strength to keep their weekend platonic.

The sensible her was thinking smart.

But the sensual her was feeling weaker by the minute.

"WE LEFT IT at that," Rory said into the phone that evening. She was upstairs in her new media room, stretched out on a chaise longue outfitted with large pillows and a chenille throw. A goblet of sparkling white wine and a ceramic bowl of hot buttered popcorn spiced with jalapeno pepper were set on a table nearby. *When Harry Met Sally,* one of her comfort movies, was in the DVD player. The remote control was at hand. Her two cats, Bogey and Bacall, were nestled in her lap.

As soon as she got off the phone with Mikki, she was done thinking about Tucker for the evening. Maybe even for the next week. She'd put him out of her mind until a reasonable way to deal with him occurred.

Yeah, right. Just the way she put Sonic burgers out of her mind after one of their commercials aired. How many times had she wound up at the drive-in with a sweater thrown on over her pj's?

"Then you *still* didn't make plans for the trip up the coast to Mendocino," Mikki said, exasperated.

"He's going to call me."

"Oh, hell."

"It wasn't like that. Not a bad-first-date 'I'll call you.' A real 'I'll call you.'"

"Nolan says—"

"We're quoting Nolan again, are we?"

"Never mind that. I got him to admit that Tucker's a total ladies' man. In all the years since Nolan and I split, Tuck's never been in a committed relationship that lasted longer than a month or two."

Rory picked up her glass of Chardonnay and took a big slug.

"I just thought I should warn you, since I've been encouraging you to go away with him, which might not be such a good idea, after all, seeing as this is *you* we're talking about, not me—"

Rory cut off the babbling, which was unlike Mikki. "Okay. Thanks for the concern. Consider me warned." *So much for the sensual side of herself entertaining thoughts of turning the weekend into a boinkathon.*

Rory flung her head against the back of the chair, managing to spill a few drops of wine on the front of her cashmere robe. "Damn," she said under her breath.

"Are you okay?"

"I'm fine and dandy. It's not as if I'm surprised. I saw from the start that Tucker has 'player' written all over him."

"Oh, come on! He's not that bad, just maybe not long-term boyfriend material. I've always adored him. After Nolan split for L.A., Tuck called often to see how I was doing. He even offered to take care of all the little fix-it jobs around the apartment, but I refused. I was in my fire-breathing, independent-feminist stage."

"Yes, I remember." Rory wondered if she should get the bottle of wine from the kitchen before she started the movie. She hated interrupting the flow of a good film with stopping-and-restarting, and she was suddenly certain that one glass wasn't enough. "I'm sure Tucker would make a great friend, but guess what? I don't want another friend."

And neither does he, she silently added, drinking more of the wine. The message from that afternoon's meeting at the construction site had been clear: Tucker could be persuaded to accommodate her needs—for one out-of-town weekend only—and damn the uncomfortable consequences that he'd mentioned earlier.

Men were so short-sighted when they started thinking with the little head.

The thought made her squeeze her thighs together, even clench her butt cheeks. She wiggled her legs. The cats stirred, blinked and dug their claws into the thick material of her robe. When she tried to pull her knees up, Bacall threw a disgusted look at her and flopped over, sprawling with her belly offered for a scratch. Rory complied, trying to distract herself from a fantasy of what she wanted to do with Tuck's nonthinking area. So maybe *she* wasn't operating on brain power, either.

"You could switch tactics," Mikki said. "Become his friend first and then—"

Rory interrupted. "I don't employ *tactics.*"

Mikki made a sound of dismissal. "For a smart woman, Rory, you really are naive. The battle of the sexes is all about gamesmanship. At least…" She paused, swallowing a shallow breath in a way that had Rory's antennae tingling. "At least until it turns into love. And sometimes even then."

They'd already mulled the past weekend's interlude with Nolan, but Mikki had maintained a flippant attitude, refusing to cop to her rising emotions even though it was obvious that Nolan had spun her world upside down.

"There are times that Nolan can be so seductive I forget why I'm mad at him," Mikki mused. "But I need to remember why our marriage broke up in the first place."

Yeah, five years ago, Rory thought, seeing the futility of keeping old wounds alive and festering. If only letting go was easier done than said, for both of them.

"Men are nothing but trouble," she announced. "Look at the trouble Lauren's having with Josh Mc-Crae."

"Did you see Lorelei's latest blog? She's on a rampage. I just about spit a mouthful of orange juice all over my laptop."

"We need to meet for coffee at Lavender Field as usual and get to the bottom of that. And just wait until you hear about the CyberCon."

"If he hurts Lauren, I'll pulverize his skull into chalk."

Rory chuckled. Mikki was fierce in love and war. "I repeat. Men are trouble."

"Mmm. Not all the time."

"No, but there's my clue. If I don't want the complications, I'm better off not getting entangled with Tucker in any way, shape or form."

Mikki should have agreed, considering her current state of marriage, but she was rarely compliant. "I don't know about that, hon. There's something to be said for entanglements."

"Like 'Yes, baby, yes, that's it, right there, you know how I like it'?"

"Were you sound-recording my weekend in Napa?" Mikki's laugh was lazy and satisfied. Also very annoying to Rory's attempt to maintain a Zen acceptance of her inadvertent celibacy.

"I'm telling you, one really good orgasm can blast out a lot of old baggage. Multiples are even more effective."

"I'll keep that in mind," Rory said dryly. "Or I could take Mom's advice and go for a high colonic instead."

"Are you kidding me? Mom's the one who first explained the value of a good screw. Remember how tranquil she was when Ahmad was courting her?"

"That was the result of sex?"

"Of course it was. You were off at college, but the noises that came out of her bedroom were almost unworldly."

"Please. No more. I'm sticking my fingers in my ears."

Mikki chided her. "If I hadn't seen you dancing with Tucker, I'd think you had no libido at all."

Rory gulped. "You saw that?"

"My face wasn't in a glass of booze the entire evening."

A moment of quiet swelled between them. Mikki tended to be very private and defensive about her struggle with alcohol, so Rory's concern usually went unspoken, though never unapparent. This time she wouldn't let the moment pass. "Mikki, sweetie, no matter what happens with Nolan, promise me you won't do that again, okay?"

After another heavy silence, Mikki sniffed. "Promise."

"Pinky swear?"

"I'll do better than that. Blood oath."

Rory's worry eased. Years ago, to solidify their sisterhood, the three of them had sworn a pinprick blood oath that they would always be there for each other. Men and arguments and unwanted advice had sometimes temporarily interfered, but they'd never ever come close to breaking the bond.

SEVERAL DAYS LATER Tucker was stretched out on a battered leather couch with the phone balanced on his stomach, staring up at the soft plaster pudding that passed for his ceiling. Needing a physical outlet even after the day's work, he'd stopped off at Nolan's office to rope his pal into a game of hoops or maybe an evening sail around the harbor.

Stupid impulse, he'd realized almost immediately, when the snobby receptionist looked at his sweaty shirt and grungy jeans as if she expected him to produce either a gun or a push broom. The attitude shouldn't have fazed him, but it did. He'd told the girl not to bother and left before his downscale presence could embarrass Nolan in front of the firm's partners.

Not that Nolan would care. He'd always been dismissive of his family's wealth. Tucker's family had the real worth, he'd said, and most of the time Tuck agreed.

But he'd taken note of the way doors that opened for Nolan never would for him, unless he went at them with a screwdriver. Didn't matter, he'd thought. Money and prestige weren't important to him.

"Lucky thing," he said with a grunt, looking around his apartment. The place was large and had several distinctive architectural features, but on first glance all a visitor would notice was how dingy and in need of major repair it was. He'd concentrated his efforts on the upstairs units to get them rented at top dollar. Living in the temporarily rundown digs had been acceptable until he'd started imagining asking a woman home for the night.

Not just any woman.

Rory.

He lifted the phone off the hook, listened to the dial tone, then replaced the handset. What the hell was he thinking? She wasn't coming to his apartment. They were having enough trouble settling on the trip to Mendocino, even with the entire weekend getaway set up for them like a goose on a silver platter.

What's the big deal? Call her, tell her you want to set a date for the trip. Maybe you'll sleep with her, maybe you won't. Either way, she's not going to expect a promise out of you. She's not as single-minded as Didi's friend, Charla. She'll see that you have no future.

That's how he liked it, right?

Not necessarily.

Not with Rory.

Could it be that she was the woman he'd been watching for? The one who would make him want to change his life—to get *ambition?*

She wasn't what he'd imagined. But she was becoming more alluring with every day he delayed.

"Nah," he said, pushing up to a sitting position. He thrust the phone onto the coffee table, not even bothering to replace the receiver when it slipped sideways.

He wasn't ready to call. Nor to answer.

He was fine the way he was, living in the present, playing his life by ear. Plans were for men in suits.

Women, too, he added, thinking of Rory at the job site, dressed for success with her sexy tailored getup and snazzy car.

She might be the woman for him, but he wasn't the man for her.

BY FRIDAY of the following week, Rory was too involved with the tasks of running her business to fret over whether or not Tucker Schulz would call. Whenever he'd crept into her mind, she'd pushed him out again and concentrated that much more on going over the gross income for last month or choosing design details for the new store. She'd managed to work her way through the final list of paint and finish choices, aware that the smallest indecision on her end would result in days or even weeks of delay at the site, putting the store's grand opening date in jeopardy. That was not going to happen.

She was energized, armed with punch lists, check-lists and to-do lists. She had more focus than the Hubble telescope.

She was horny as hell.

Katya poked her head inside Rory's office. "Julio brought over some of the new focaccia for us to sample."

"Uh-huh."

"You told me to drag you out of the office if you said 'uh-huh.'"

"In a minute."

"You told me to bean you in the head with a baguette if you said 'In a minute.'"

Rory looked up from her lists. "But you're too nice, right?"

"Nope. We're sold out of baguettes. Business has been wild, with the gay pride parade this weekend."

"I know. That's why I've been hiding in my office."

"It's only three and we're practically down to crumbs."

"Have you called around to the other stores to see if they can send us their overage?"

"I tried." Katya wagged her frizzy head. She was in her late thirties, a lean, energetic single mother of three who'd started at Lavender Field as a baker because the early morning shift meant she could be home for her kids during the day. They were all in school now, and Rory had promoted Katya to manager when she no longer had the time to keep track of day-to-day operations. "The other stores are practically sold out, too."

Rory reached for the phone. "We'd better up our order for this weekend."

"Already did that."

She set down the phone. "You're the best."

Katya buffed her nails on the front of the eyelet-trimmed apron. "Are you coming then?"

"Uh-huh."

"I almost forgot. There's a customer asking if you're available. His name is, uh…"

Rory's head snapped up. "Tucker?"

"No. I want to say George, but that's not it, either. He's been in before. Big and bald? Suit and tie?"

"Oh, him." Rory took a couple of seconds for her adrenaline to drop back. Pavlov's dog had nothing on her. "That's this guy I met at the key party. I think I'll stay here and avoid him."

"Don't you like bald men? I mean, you saw *Pitch Black* about ten times, you actually liked *Alien^3*, and you had that *Anna and the King* party where we all had to wear skull caps in honor of Yul Brenner…"

"Wasn't the Persian feast worth it?"

"Chow Yun Fat was worth it. Even though he's not bald."

"Yeah." Rory smiled with fond memories of the dance scene. She was a sucker for romantic moments, modest, grand or anywhere in between. "I forgave him."

"I'd better get back." Katya hesitated in the doorway. "Don't wait too long. The bread will be all gone."

"Save me a slice." Rory waved the manager away, but after a minute she abandoned hope of continuing with work. Her concentration was shot. Even the possibility of Tucker asking for her was a sliver under her skin. She had to worry at the thought until he'd been successfully removed.

Did she want to sit around, stewing about a man who was in absolutely no rush to see her again?

Hell no.

Rory got up from the desk and went to eat bread. Julio was one of her best bakers and he'd been working on coming up with an even tastier focaccia, experimenting with flavor combinations. She had a mouthful of a heavenly apple and caramelized onion bread when a man's voice spoke her name.

"Hey, Rory. I hope you don't mind me coming back here."

She whirled. Tucker.

Her mouth was full. She thrust out the hand with the bread. "Focaccia?" she said thickly, trying to chew and swallow at the same time.

He blinked. "What?"

She took a big gulp and the lump of half-chewed bread went down her throat. "Focaccia?"

"Oh. Focaccia! Whew. Thought you said something else." Grinning, he put out his hand. "I love a good focaccia."

She gave him a slice of the bread along with a baleful stare, even though laughter brimmed at her lips. "What happened to George, or whatever his name is?"

"Big Baldy? He suddenly remembered that he had an appointment."

"Uh-huh."

"This is great bread."

"Isn't it?" She helped herself to a different slice and

tasted subtle hints of sage and sea salt. Julio had left several of the flat loaves on the butcher-block work-table, which had been cleared off and scrubbed down by the on-site bakers, who'd all departed for the day. "Did you come by the store for anything special? We're running low on stock, but I can offer you a dozen of our frozen garlic cheese sticks. Stick them in the oven for ten minutes and they'll melt your taste buds off."

"Thanks, but I'm good. Hearing you say focaccia was all I needed."

This time she laughed. "Don't get your hopes up. Focacci-ya isn't the same as focacci-me."

Tucker leaned against the butcher block with both elbows and took a leisurely look around the kitchen be-fore his gaze returned to her face. "You sure about that?"

She merely smiled, uncertain about how to respond. His tanned muscular forearms were pressed against the worktop, hands clasped. They were working man's hands, strong and competent. Clean, clipped nails, no ornamentation.

And she was getting hot at the sight of them.

For an instant she closed her eyes, but when she opened them her gaze went to the gap at the small of his back where his T-shirt was tucked into belted jeans. Suddenly she was unable to suppress the thought of slipping one hand inside to do a little kneading of his buns.

Good God! What had Julio baked into his bread to get her so worked up? Next thing, she'd be ripping her blouse open and asking Tucker to roll around on a flour-dusted butcher block à la *The Postman Always Rings Twice.*

She dry-swallowed. "You must have had a reason for stopping by."

"I was curious to see your store." He straightened, once more checking out the industrial-size, stainless-steel mixers and stoves.

To give the place a French country feel, she'd added yellow-print curtains, dried flowers and herbs and open shelves that held a mismatched collection of china and pottery, bought cheap at French flea markets. Ever since a semester abroad in Paris had changed her life, she'd made yearly sojourns to France, even during the time when going meant taking a backpack and staying in youth hostels.

She brushed the bread crumbs into a tiny pile. "And?"

"And it suddenly struck me. Our weekend in Mendocino will work out a lot better if we're comfortable with each other as friends before we go."

She kept her gaze low. One of his arms was braced against the butcher block, delineating the cords and veins. "I suppose you're right."

"Do you want to go to the movies? We still have the movie passes we won."

"I forgot about those." First time in her life she'd put off going to the cinema. "What do you mean, like right now?"

"Sure. We can see a matinee."

A matinee. Because they were *friends.*

"I'm working," she said.

He dimpled. "Phone in an excuse."

"But I'm the boss."

"I know."

"What about you? Don't you have to work?"

"I quit early."

She cocked her head. "Do you do that a lot?" Not very dependable.

Her work ethic was strong. When she was ten, Emma had started her doing household chores for rewards, such as a movie matinee for just the two of them, a rare respite from the constant demands of her foster charges. Rory had been earning her own spending money from the time she was thirteen and had held a variety of odd jobs until she'd graduated and signed on as a city social worker. Burnout and a return to weekly bread-baking therapy with her mother had led to the opening of the first Lavender Field.

"My hours are flexible," Tucker said. "Unless I have an emergency situation, I can leave when the mood strikes me." He shrugged as if the idea of being responsible was of no consequence. "So what do you say?"

Reminding herself that she was making a snap judgment, she stored her comments on his seeming irresponsibility for another time. "Can I pick the movie?"

"I'm allergic to chick flicks."

She smiled. "You'd do anything for a friend, wouldn't you?"

For a couple of seconds he turned sober. The regard in his mossy-colored eyes gave her insides a squeeze.

She was getting ready to capitulate when he said, "All right, you win. Lead me to Julia Roberts."

"Wonderful." On impulse, she took his hand, wondering if she could lead them both into temptation instead.

6

RORY TOOK HIM to her favorite local movie house, where she'd said the monster buckets didn't outsize the screens. She'd asked for only a diet drink, but he had purchased a tub of popcorn, too, certain that he could tempt her with it. When they'd walked in, she'd taken a deep breath with a look of utter satisfaction on her face.

The expression had been inspiring. He'd imagined giving her that look through means of his own and ninety percent of his blood had immediately rushed below the Mason-Dixon line.

Damn. There was no bottling the chemistry between them. His offer to be her friend for the day hadn't been a lie, but not the whole truth, either. He'd wanted to meet her on neutral ground to see where they stood. No ground was neutral enough.

They were early for the movie. After Rory had chosen optimal seating and they'd arranged themselves, they sat in silence for a minute before both spoke at once.

"So, tell me about—"

"What's this movie—"

They exchanged smiles. "You go first," he said, offering her the popcorn.

She picked out a single kernel. "Since we're getting to know each other as friends, I was going to ask about your family. You mentioned a couple of older sisters?"

"Didi and Jenny. Both married with kids. Didi's a comic book editor and Jenny's a stay-at-home mom, living at my parents'. You'd like both of them, but especially Didi. She's the bossy one."

"Oh, yeah? Do you think I'm bossy?"

"You have that big-sister aura."

"Bossy," she said, with a humorous inflection.

"Maybe so. Except I've never heard Mikki complain. You're probably the only person she'll listen to without bristling."

"Oh, she bristles plenty. But she does listen. Also to Lauren and our mother, Emma. Especially Emma."

"You call your mother by her first name?"

"Often. She's that type. Very…oh, you know—democratic."

"I don't think I've ever met her."

"You'd remember if you had." Rory frowned slightly, then lifted her shoulders in a quick sigh. "Emma was on vacation in South America when Mikki eloped, so she missed the wedding party I th—"

Rory stopped in midstream, looking embarrassed. He sat straighter, studying her in the low house lights. "What did you say? I'm missing something here."

She rattled the ice in her cup, then took a long sip from the straw, glancing around the theater. Another dozen or so moviegoers had arrived and were chattering and noshing as they waited for the show to begin.

"Rory?"

"Oh, all right. I might as well tell you." Her drink went into the cup holder. She looked him in the eye. "We've met before, right after Mikki and Nolan eloped."

"I don't remember you."

"Obviously. Do you remember the wedding party?"

"Yes…"

"That was at my apartment. My sister Lauren and I hosted it."

"So that's why she looked familiar," he blurted.

Rory raised her brows at him, then faced front as the lights dimmed and the previews began.

He was an idiot. "I meant—"

She cut him off. "Forget it."

"Look, that was a long time ago. Do you remember *me* from the party?"

"Shh. I like to watch the trailers." She scrunched down in her seat.

He scrunched, too. Grasping at straws, he whispered, "That party was a madhouse. The entire evening's a blur."

"Don't worry about it. I was different then."

"How so?"

She pointed at the screen. "Shh."

"We'll talk about this later," he said.

Her profile remained cool and steady. He stared at the flickering screen for a few minutes without being able to follow the rapid-shot editing of the trailer for yet another end-of-the-world sci-fi thriller.

The tension radiating from Rory was as prickly as static electricity. Wary of the shock if he touched her, but willing to take the chance, he shifted the popcorn bucket and took her hand in his.

She stiffened.

He squeezed. "I'm sorry I didn't remember you."

Her eyes glistened in the light off the screen as she slowly turned her face to him. She leaned closer so he could hear her hushed voice. "It's okay. Most women don't like to think they're forgettable, but I'm kind of used to it. Don't give it another thought. We'd been serving piña coladas. You probably had one too many."

Except that after a fashion he'd remembered Lauren. Rory's spot in his memory was shamefully blank. He hated the idea that he'd dismissed her because she didn't fit some lame stereotype of the California blonde. Even worse—he'd done it twice. He'd barely given her a look at the key party until they'd been thrown together and there'd been no avoiding conversation.

She'd held his attention *then*. And he'd been fighting the attraction ever since.

Why?

Granted, he was a fairly simple guy who hadn't seen need to question the standard idea of beauty. When it came to women, he acted on instinct and impulse. But he wasn't shallow—or so he'd thought. Looks weren't the only component in his sexual attraction to Rory. Even if they were, she'd do fine.

She tried to remove her hand, but he wouldn't let her. "Maybe this is fate," he said with his mouth near her ear. "I wasn't ready to meet you—*really* meet you—back then."

Her gaze remained pinned to the screen. "Sweet talk," she said out of the side of her mouth.

"Just buttering you up."

She reached over and scooped up a handful of popcorn. "You're not a movie talker, are you? Because I'm warning you right now, I'm a serious film buff and if you start asking me questions or making inane comments, I'm liable to dump this bucket of popcorn over your head."

"I won't say a word."

She shot him a suspicious glance, then popped several kernels into her mouth. "Mumph. We'll see if you can be good."

"Hey." He stroked his thumb over the back of her hand. "I never promised *that.*"

"FINALLY I've disarmed you," the bounty hunter cooed as she stripped down to a skimpy tank and a thong the size of an eye patch. The hefty knife strapped to her thigh covered more skin than her undergarments.

The leading man turned beneath the pounding shower spray, a long, tall slab of wet man that made Rory's tongue curl. She sank even lower in her seat, tightening up to stop from squirming so Tucker wouldn't know the scene was giving her ants in her pants.

The movie hero flashed a charming grin remarkably like Tucker's. "I may be disarmed, but I'm still packing heat."

Rory caught her tongue between her teeth as the screen couple kissed, their sculpted bodies lit to a honeyed glow. Her fingers dug into the armrests. Torture. She'd thought an action picture would be safe, but she should have stuck with her first intention of seeing a chick flick. At least the sex in them was usually of the lighthearted farcical type.

Tucker was watching her. Though she hadn't taken her gaze from the screen, but she could see him in her peripheral vision.

Looking amused.

Great. He probably thought she was embarrassed.

By a little bit of screen steam? Ha! She was made of sterner stuff than that.

Her elbow nudged him. "Ever done it in a shower?"

Tucker's head cocked.

"I was just wondering—does that work? I picture crashing through the shower door or skidding on the wet porcelain."

"Then you must have a very *active* imagination."

She made a noncommittal sound, but the answer was, *Hell, yes.*

"Do you imagine us together?" he whispered.

"Well, yes…sometimes," she admitted.

He touched her chin with a couple of fingers, gently turning her face even when she resisted. She gave in. The intimacy of being close to him in the darkness, of feeling his breath on her cheek and the rush of potent desire, was too delicious to fight.

"I thought you didn't talk during movies," he said.

"Oops."

"Since we're breaking rules…"

His placed his lips against hers, with a feathery grace that surprised her. She hadn't expected him to be subtle. Maybe he was being cautious.

The warmth of his mouth was inviting. She opened hers, just a little, the tip of her tongue pressing between her teeth. They twisted in their seats, her hand catching at his arm, his fingers sliding from beneath her chin to burrow into her hair. He cupped her head, the motion deepening their kiss naturally as their tongues stroked and teased.

Pleasure sifted through Rory like salt sprinkled on popcorn. Her hand opened and closed on the flexing muscles in Tucker's upper arm. He reached around her waist, pulling her tight. She wanted to climb right out of her seat—her *clothes*—and into his lap.

His kiss was playful. But thorough. Every inch of her was tingling long before he was finished. Her nipples had gone hard beneath the trappings of her sturdy underwire bra. She wished to feel his hands on them, to press herself against his chest, but the theater seats were conducive only for the make-out sessions of flexible teenagers. She couldn't be that brazen, anyway…could she?

Tucker's hand had found its way to the side of her breast, thank goodness. His kisses moved from her mouth to her neck. Panting, she nudged him with her arm. He hadn't needed the direction. His fingers were already curved over the swell of her breast. The pad of his thumb pressed down hard on the nipple, rolling it back and forth. Pleasure melted into heat, so sizzling she had to let out it out in a moan, loud enough for the entire audience to hear.

Embarrassment streaked through her. Tucker only smiled and leaned in for another kiss.

She put her hands against his chest, holding him away. "Slow down, cowboy. We're in the middle of the theater." She *would* choose the best seats in the place instead of a darker, private corner.

"No one cares."

"I do."

"I can tell," he said, his face close beside hers in the dark, and suddenly she realized that his hand was *under* her blouse, his fingers slipping up beneath the elastic of her bra to sweep over her right breast, working back and forth over her aching nipple. Delicious sensation shot through her and she caught her breath, holding back another moan.

He nibbled on her ear. "Relax. No one can see what we're doing."

She slumped, knowing she should stop him, but there was too much pleasure. He stroked her, making her body soft with desire and hard with excitement. The illicit location only added to her thrill, and suddenly she understood why Lauren used to see so many movies with her high-school boyfriend.

Tucker had slipped down the cup of her bra and popped a few buttons on her blouse. Her bared breast was practically spilling out. She turned toward him—for cover, but also as an offering. Her inhibitions were rapidly becoming the equivalent of the pool of leftover butter flavoring at the bottom of the popcorn bucket.

They kissed. His palm covered her breast, merely holding her when she wanted more. She made an encouraging sound and rolled her shoulders, opening her mouth, licking at his hot tongue.

"More," she urged under her breath, using her arm to keep his hand tight against her.

He fingered her nipple. A purely sexual shiver ran through her. *Okay! I can do this.*

"More?" He removed his mouth from hers and took in a deep breath. "Let's get out of here then."

Oh, boy. Could she do this *right now?*

"And miss the movie?" she blurted as she glanced up at the screen. The muscular hero and the sexy bounty hunter were climbing down a fire escape in their skivvies while the bad guy shot at them from above.

Tucker grinned broadly, his teeth pearly in the darkness. "I've lost track of the plot."

"It's not like this movie requires a brain," she said, stalling to give herself time to think.

Think? Not when her body was sending whacked-out messages to her brain. Telling her to do such things as grab him, kiss him, crawl onto her knees in front of him and take his hot erection into her mouth…

Ohmygawd. She shuddered mightily, her eyes glued to the screen as she pulled her blouse shut. *I cannot do this!*

Tucker's arm was still looped across her midriff, his hand positioned beneath her breast. He didn't move it even when she wriggled, which meant she couldn't fix her bra, which meant her nipple remained pointed and tingling, stark evidence that indeed she could have done more if she'd dared.

"What happened to just being friends?" she hissed.

Someone several rows back told her to hush. Rory shrank into her seat. Only once had she been disruptive at a movie theater—as a teenager, the time Lauren and Mikki had started a popcorn war with some cute surfer dudes several rows down and they'd all been asked to leave. The two sides had met on the sidewalk in front of the theater and paired up almost instantly, with some unerring instinct that Rory had seemed to lack. She'd held back, watching Mikki flirt, aware that the third male of the trio was looking at her with less than enthusiasm.

That had been years ago. She shouldn't even remember the incident.

"We can still be friends afterward," Tucker whispered.

"But we might also be family," she pointed out.

"So we'll be kissing cousins."

She sighed. "That won't work."

He didn't respond for several minutes. When she thought she was safe again, he said, "Are you sure?" and removed his arm.

Not in the least. An attraction like this one didn't come around often enough for her to dismiss it casually, with anything resembling certainty. Especially when sexual hunger was still running in her veins, telling her to grab a bite of Tucker.

But she nodded.

"Uhm." Tucker picked up the tub of popcorn he'd set aside and held it over his lap.

What did *uhm* mean? She looked down, then up at his strained expression. Oh.

After ten minutes of onscreen shooting and running and fireball explosions, when she was sure that his arousal had modified, she dug a hand into the popcorn bucket and started shoving the greasy treat into her mouth without concern for spotting her silk blouse. She needed something to chew on—other than him.

"HERE'S WHAT we do—"

"I'll have a latte," Rory said, her chin in her hand as she studied the chalkboard menu hung near the ceiling.

"Nothing to eat?"

"I'm full of popcorn. Don't report me to the nutrition police, but that was my dinner."

Tucker told the guy behind the counter they'd have two coffees. "We need to make a decision. Obviously there's something between us."

"Yes. A table." She splayed her hands over the Formica. "That is, a counter." There were no tables, only a row of bar stools.

He shook his head. They were in his favorite eatery, a shoebox-shaped diner that was little more than a run-down fish shack, but also a city landmark for fifty years. A couple of times a week, he stopped by for clam chowder or a plate of oysters.

The smell of fresh catch hung in the air as thickly as the fog that rolled along the nearby piers. "You're not taking this seriously," he said.

She shrugged. "Thought I'd try something different."

Her eyes betrayed a certain wariness about the reversal of their positions, as if she found him confusing. Negotiating a relationship with Rory, even a temporary one, was a complex issue.

Two mugs were plunked down in front of them. Tuck took his time, stirring two sugars into his coffee. "You're doing this to torment me, aren't you?"

"You have all those older brothers and sisters. You must be used to it."

"Doesn't mean I like it." And his feelings for her weren't familial, so she could drop that line of defense right now.

"You're cute," she said, being indulgent.

"I'm not a puppy."

"If you were, you'd be a beagle. Happy, friendly, sporting. Short velvet fur."

He rubbed a couple of fingers inside his collar. "Floppy ears? Cold nose?"

"And those imploring eyes…"

"Wait," he said. Damn that movie. At Rory's insistence, they'd stayed through the credits, effectively dowsing the lingering effects of their make-out session. He knew he could ratchet the desire back on high with only a few intimate caresses, but Rory was determined not to let him.

Over the rim of her mug, she looked at him. She was fully aware of their chemistry. As much as she was pretending otherwise.

"You think I'm begging?" he asked.

"Maybe a little."

His gaze dropped to her breasts, pressed together between her arms which were resting on the counter.

Two small bumps showed through her silky shirt. When her nipples started to harden even more, she bent her elbows, lacing her fingers into a cradle for her chin and maintaining her fake I'm-not-turned-on expression.

You're not fooling me, he said in silence. *I've touched you there and I know how much you liked it.*

He sipped the hot brew, grinning inside at his own bouts with denial when it came to Rory. Despite the latest attempt, he was officially admitting—if only to himself—that he wanted to see her naked. Wanted it more every time they were together. The wanting had become so important that it was actually a good reason to keep away.

But he just couldn't do that.

"Here's what we do," he said. "We head north to Painter's Cove, and if we end up in bed together that's okay—" Hell, it was more than okay. It was vital. "And if we don't, that's fine, too. We'll be friends either way, right?"

"Right." She frowned.

"Your mouth says right but your eyes say wrong."

She flicked the smooth, blunt ends of her hair off one shoulder. "As a rule, I don't do casual sex."

"I don't do it with rules, either."

"Now who's being flippant?"

"You're right. This is getting us nowhere."

Her eyes darkened. "Maybe *nowhere* is where we should be."

The heavy thud of disappointment in his chest went ignored. He said with a clenched jaw, "We could give the weekend away. Maureen would know a single mother, someone who'd really appreciate the getaway."

Rory nodded. "That would be the smart and generous thing to do."

He looked at her lips and didn't feel like being noble. Or smart. "Then again…"

"It's not like I haven't done my share when it comes to charity work. Emma raised me right."

"I gave at the office," he said.

"And we did buy our tickets, like everyone else. We're entitled."

"So we're back on?"

She nodded. "I am if you are."

"When?"

"I have interviews next week. I'm hiring for the positions in my new store. And there's the work being done there—the contractor is always demanding my input." She slid a PDA from her purse and tapped the buttons with the tip of her nail, calling up a calendar. "How about the last weekend in June? Would that work with your schedule?"

"No problem."

She looked up. "Mmm, yes. I forgot. Tradesmen never seem to have a problem with disappearing off a job at a moment's notice."

"I don't run my business that way."

She didn't seem to believe him. "Well, lots do. This is the fourth store I've renovated and even though I have a good contractor, we still get delays."

"Who's subbing the electrical?"

Back to the PDA. "Scully and Sons."

"Never heard of them."

"It's a big city. I think they're new. New to me, anyway. My old electrician retired." She named a name that Tuck approved of.

"Next time, hire me," he said.

"You're good?"

"Very good."

Pink tinged her cheeks. "We'll see. I'll need to get a taste of your work. Make sure you live up to your reputation."

"I have a reputation?"

"Mikki says you do."

Tuck narrowed his gaze. "Who's she been talking to?"

"Nolan," Rory said with a laugh.

"You can't listen to that guy. For a smart lawyer, he's awfully dumb. Didn't even know he was married."

Rory sobered. "I hope they make it."

"Easier for us if they don't."

"Easy?"

"Y'know—if we hook up."

"It's not the hook-up I'm worried about. It's the unhooking that'll cause problems." She rolled her bottom lip between her teeth, staring at the electronic device held between her hands. "Are you one of those guys who wants to stay friends afterward?"

"Not exactly. But I don't want to make enemies, either. Especially not with you."

He waited a minute, but she didn't respond. "How about you?" he asked, guessing that she would worry over every little detail of what might happen. Mikki had referred to her sister as a mother hen.

"I want everyone to like me." She sighed. "It's my curse."

"That's not a curse."

"When you take it too far, yes it is. I have a large circle of friends, plus I keep in touch with a number of my foster brothers and sisters. Several of them work at my stores, in fact."

"But what about your exes?"

"Well…" She stalled. "It seems that there aren't as many of those. In general, yes, they still count as friends. If I liked a man enough to be in a relationship, I usually like him even after the breakup." She winced. "Depending on the breakup."

Aha. She'd been badly hurt. Being the kind of woman who took such things to heart, that explained her excessive caution.

A red light clicked on in Tucker's brain, where normally he saw nothing but green. Messing with Rory would be a very dumb move, especially since he couldn't see one weekend getaway expanding into a full-fledged affair. He'd have to decide if risking a possible friendship was worth a couple of days of what promised to be some pretty hot sex.

Damn. Normally he'd take the sex and worry about the other tomorrow. Why'd he ever come up with the idea that they needed to be friends first? Not to mention that all this second-guessing was digging him into a deep hole, the very thing he wanted to avoid.

"I'm not a clinger, if that's what you're thinking with your worried puppy-dog frown. I have my pride," she said in a low voice.

"I can see that."

He studied her eyes, beer-bottle amber, flecked with gold and dark brown. He knew only a little about her, but one thing he'd realized was that she had no idea of her beauty. He'd had no idea, either, at first. Her appeal was the kind that sneaked up on a guy, gaining luster with every conversation. The more he knew her, the prettier she got…and the deeper he slid. She was the female equivalent of quicksand.

Red light.

Yet here he was, gunning for their weekend, all systems on go.

TUCKER WAITED impatiently outside the Hibraugh School of Art. The plan was that Rory would meet him after her Friday afternoon art class and they'd drive up to Mendocino in her convertible. He'd had a long four-and-a-half days of work, trying to finish the rewiring job on a Russian Hill reno. He was ready for a weekend of pure relaxation.

Probably not what he was gonna get.

He scanned the parking lot, then the building. No sign of Rory or her car.

He checked his watch. Maybe he had the time wrong.

Inaction drove him crazy, and this thing with Rory had been all about inaction up to now. They'd had a number of telephone conversations in the past few weeks and he'd acquired the habit of stopping in at Lavender Field the last couple of Saturday mornings to say hello and to pick up a loaf of bread or a couple dozen sourdough rolls for Sunday dinner at his parents'. Mikki and Lauren were usually there, chattering with Rory over coffee and croissants. The suggestion that they take the long convertible trip up the coast to Mendocino had been theirs, though neither he nor Rory had put up much objection.

Tuck picked up his gym bag and slung the strap over his shoulder. He was antsy, done with talking and planning.

So let's just do it.

He went into the building, found a roster of classes pinned to a message board in the lobby and took the flight of stairs two at a time. Rory's class should be ending any minute now. He'd hurry her along so they could get out of the city before the late-afternoon traffic jammed up.

Life drawing was in the studio on the north side of the building. A flood of students swarmed through the hallway as a couple of other classes concluded. Tucker went against the flow and found the room, surprised to see that the door's glass inset was taped over with brown paper.

He waited for a minute, listening. Silence within.

Wrong studio? He knocked lightly, then opened the door. Several artists looked up from easels arranged in a semicircle.

Tucker cleared his throat. "Is this the li—"

Belatedly he realized what he was seeing. He stood frozen, his eyes widened, unable to fully take in the sight in front of him.

A nude woman was posing on a dais in the center of the room.

That in itself wasn't so shocking.
What truly did him in was her identity.
Rory Constable.
Totally, unabashedly, spectacularly *nude*.

7

IMPOSSIBLE, but true. Tucker couldn't seem to absorb it, even while his eyes gobbled up the sight.

Aurora Constable, savvy businesswoman, best friend, modest soul...*nude, from head to toe.*

Her back was to him. But the sight was still hot enough to singe his lashes.

She lounged on a padded, fabric-draped bench, legs pulled up, leaning to the side on her arm so that her body formed a lazy *S,* a shape designed for an artistic eye and talented fingers. In one fell swoop, she embodied everything that he loved about a womanly shape—the lush sensuality, the comfortable curves and supple skin, the smooth elegance.

She was so pale she had an almost incandescent glow. A poet might have used words such as ivory and moonlight, but Tuck could only repeat one word over and over in his head. Wow.

Wow wow wow wow.

Her ass was bountiful perfection. Her waist was small, or at least small in comparison to the flare of her hips. The tilt of her upper body and the angle of her arm gave him a provocative view of the side of a full—very full—breast.

That was where his stare stalled out. He'd never seen a more tantalizing sight than the teasing view of Rory's breast. He'd have paid a million dollars for the pleasure of watching her slowly turn to face him.

But she didn't move. Not even to turn her head.

Tucker found his bearings. Clenching his fists, he walked into the room, hell-bent on completing his artistic encounter. Only a couple of seconds had passed since he'd opened the door, but they'd last forever in his memory.

A woman approached. He couldn't be bothered.

She held up a hand. "Excuse me, sir…"

He didn't stop. "Is this the life drawing class?"

"Yes it is. But we don't allow visitors."

The artists had continued sketching, unperturbed. Tuck glanced at one of the charcoal drawings. The figure on the paper was recognizable as a nude, but not as Rory in particular. Although he was no judge of art, the drawing was nowhere near as good as the real thing.

He'd gained the front view. Rory's chin was high. Her eyes were closed. Her breasts…ah, her breasts. They were opulent. Even better than he'd imagined. Centerfold breasts, except they were real, tipped by large nipples the color of café au lait.

"Sir? This is a private class. You *must* leave."

"Yeah," he said, not moving. Staring.

"We don't allow gawkers." The woman snatched up a robe hung over the back of a chair and headed toward the dais, holding the garment up to shield Rory.

Rory finally opened her eyes. They were an arrow tipped in golden flame, aimed straight at Tucker.

He had no defense.

"It's all right, Sukie." Rory's voice was utterly calm. "He's with me."

She astounded him at every turn.

The woman, Sukie, grumbled at him, but she dropped the robe. She was petite with a lined face and silver dandelion-fluff hair. After glaring at Tucker once more, she checked the time of a clock on the wall and said, "Class, you have three minutes to finish."

Pencils moved faster, making scratching sounds on paper.

Tuck wished he was an artist.

A sculptor. He could run his hands over Rory's naked flesh, explore those lavish curves. Her belly was softly rounded. As he watched, she pressed her thighs closer together, luring his gaze along her carefully arranged legs. They were long, shapely, with trim ankles and polished toes. He hadn't fully realized just how incredible they were.

Blood pounded, thickening in his groin. He was back in school, getting the instant, uncontrollable hard-on of a teenager.

Rory would see. He shoved his hands into the front pockets of his jeans, turning in a casual circle as if he wanted to scan the studio for interesting art.

When he looked back, she had her eyes closed again. In case this was his only chance, he feasted on the sight of her, willing to risk a zipper-splitting erection for the pleasure.

She was absolute perfection.

Hard to believe that the art students were so blasé

about their nude model. Several of them were men. Tuck studied their faces, but they gave away nothing, seemingly more interested in their drawings than Rory.

Hell. She might believe they were detached, but he didn't. No man could be unaffected by the sight. Her nudity was flagrantly sexual. Unless they were gay, the men in the class were accumulating fantasy fodder for years to come.

A protective jealousy surged through Tucker. Now *he* wanted to throw that robe across her.

"Time's up," the teacher said. She began making a tour of the drawings, commenting on each of them, giving pointers on what could be improved.

Rory broke her pose, swinging her legs down off the bench. The shadowed triangle at the top of her thighs shifted, and Tucker found himself moving at Superman speed, grabbing the robe and holding it out for her as she stepped down.

Instead of immediately covering herself the way he'd expected, she stopped before him, ignoring the dangling sleeves. He wondered if the previous modesty was an act and she actually enjoyed shedding her clothing in public. She might be a nudist. Maybe an exhibitionist. Her upbringing had been unconventional, with that kooky mother and the house filled with a ragtag band of foster kids. Anything was possible.

He came from a fairly conservative Catholic background, but you couldn't live in San Francisco and not be accepting of a wide range of lifestyles.

Rory was an enigma. Fortunately he had three days with her to discover her secrets. And all her secret places.

"Hello, Tucker," she said, staring him full in the face. Her eyes were bright and held open a little too wide. If not for that and the spotty color in her cheeks, he'd have thought she was completely unembarrassed.

He waggled the robe.

Her lips curved as she slid her arms into the deep kimono sleeves. "You surprised me."

"*I* surprised *you?*"

She gave an airy laugh. Reaching for it, he thought.

"This is why I told you to meet me outside," she chided.

Although she held the robe closed across her breasts, it still hung loose. He fumbled for the fabric belt, pulling and tying it tightly around her waist.

"I got tired of waiting." He tugged at the belt to be sure it was secure.

Her shoulders jerked, making her breasts sway beneath the silky material. Dear God. He couldn't take much more of this.

"I'm sorry about barging in," he added, even though he wasn't.

Rory snorted. She wasn't one to hold back her reactions. "The name of the class didn't give you a clue?"

"Life drawing? I didn't think about it. For all I knew, you'd be drawing a bowl of fruit."

"That's a still life."

She was not still. She jiggled and swayed, her body loose and free under the robe as she bent slightly to slip her feet into a pair of thong sandals with low heels.

"The class should be called nude drawing," he said, struggling to keep his hands off her.

The students were gathering together their gear, calling out goodbyes, offering their thanks to Rory and the teacher. One of the women jokingly mentioned getting to the gym before it was her turn.

"Or at least figure drawing," Tucker added. "Give a man some warning."

Rory straightened. "You could have been a gentleman and turned your back when you saw I was modeling."

"Never occurred to me." He smoothed the fold in her lapel, weakening enough to allow himself to run his finger down the seam, toward her cleavage.

She caught his hand, holding it tightly above her breasts. Her racing heartbeat gave him another clue that she was not as calm as she'd strived to appear. "Are you teasing me?" she asked.

He lowered his mouth near her ear. "That was a compliment."

"I know." Her voice had dropped several registers, so deep and throaty it quickened his already indecent arousal. One step closer and his hard-on would brush her thigh. She'd have tangible proof that the friends-first experiment had gone out the window as soon as he'd seen her posing in her birthday suit.

"Why were you modeling?" he asked. "I thought you were a student."

Her color heightened. "Nude models are expensive. So we take turns."

He glanced at the departing students. The teacher hovered near the front of the room, watching him. "Really? Everyone? Isn't that sort of scandalous?"

"Not at all. We're artists. We see shadows, contour and form, not breasts and penises."

"Gotta say, I'm skeptical. Tell me you don't feel any personal interest from the male students when you're stretched out naked in front of them."

"Not really. Granted, it was strange at first. But we try to be serious about it, and, well, I'm usually more concerned with keeping my own cool than worrying about what the others are thinking."

"Keeping your cool," he mused. "Does that mean public nudity excites you?"

Vigorous headshake. She seemed appalled at the suggestion. "How could you say that? You don't know me at all."

"I *thought* I knew you. Then I walked in here and—" He gestured, words failing him.

"Uh, Rory?" called the teacher. "I can give you a few more minutes, but after that I'll be late for my Kabbalah class."

Rory glanced around the emptied studio. "Oh, right. Sorry, Sukie. I was distracted." She shot another measuring glance Tucker's way, a wicked little smile turning up the corners of her mouth. "We're leaving. Just let me get my things and I'll go and change in the bathroom."

"Can I help?" he asked.

She collected her belongings—a large purse patterned with a repeating designer label and a neat pile of folded clothing. "You can take my drawing pad and pencil box out to the car. I'll join you in a minute."

They left the studio, with Sukie locking up after

them. Rory disappeared into the ladies' room. Tucker decided to wait. He might not be a gentleman when it came to passing up semipublic displays of naked breasts, but he wouldn't leave her to walk out alone, either.

He leaned against the wall, idly paging through Rory's sketches. She'd been straight with him: the drawings were of her fellow students, both clothed and unclothed. They flipped by in all shapes, sizes and ages. There was something equalizing about the humble display of human flesh.

Maybe she was right about that, too. He found none of the sketches particularly arousing, even the one of a Latina bombshell who'd posed like Xena, Warrior Princess.

It was the sight of Rory he couldn't forget. Which meant her naked body had a unique significance for him.

He wanted her so bad that he was screwed before he'd actually been screwed.

Rory came out minutes later, smoothing her hair back from her face, a piece of knotted leather stuck in her mouth. She removed the leather band and used it to anchor her ponytail. "You're still here."

He tucked the sketch pad under his arm and ran his eyes over her unzipped jacket and the clinging tank top beneath it. "I decided to wait. You look almost as good when you're dressed."

Damn. He'd thought that the few minutes apart would help, but her naked self was back—smack-dab center in his mind's eye. He'd probably never be able to look at her again without remembering.

Worth the distraction, he decided. Because he'd been let in on an intimate secret: unlike most people, Rory Constable looked best in the nude.

She crinkled her nose. "Thanks, I guess."

"That was a compliment, too."

She tugged on the drawstring of her pants. "This is so weird."

"Why? Because I saw you naked?"

She groaned.

"You can see me naked, if you want to even things up."

"Oh?"

"I'll even pose for you."

"Watch out. I might take you up on that."

"My pleasure," he said, thinking of how he could make it so they both ended up unclothed at the same time. He grabbed his duffel off the floor. "Let's get out of here. We've got a long drive ahead of us and suddenly I can't wait to see what Painter's Cove has in store for us."

"SERIOUSLY NOW, explain to me about the posing."

"Tucker! Not again. Why are you so stuck on that?"

"I can't get it out of my head."

It? Rory wondered. Certainly he meant *her.* But was that good or bad?

"You're not even trying," she said.

"Why should I?" He gave her a devilish grin before wadding up the empty Doritos bag from her supply of road-trip snacks. He tossed the crumpled ball into the back seat and slouched lower in his seat, his eyes hidden behind a pair of dark sunglasses. "Pretend I'm an art connoisseur."

Uh-huh. T-and-A connoisseur was more like it, Rory thought, but she held her tongue. Better to steer the conversation to less risky—and risqué—avenues.

Not so easy. They were two hundred miles north of San Francisco on Highway 101 and she still couldn't get the incident at the art studio out of her head, either. While it might have been preferable, and certainly safer, to assume that Tucker had thought her body was average at best, she wasn't allowing herself to get caught in the self-doubting trap.

The truth had been there in his eyes—he'd thought she'd looked very good. Of course, her appeal was of the voluptuous Renoir sort, but that was okay. So what if her shape wasn't fashionably skinny? There were a lot of men who appreciated a full-figured woman.

Ugh. Full-figured sounded really staid.

Curvy, then. She was a woman with dangerous curves.

Rory wanted to glance at Tucker again, but the road was twisting, following the contours of the scenic coastline. To her left, spectacular ocean vistas beckoned, dramatic with crashing waves and rugged cliffs. Manzanita clung to the rocks in twisted forms, redwood and cypress trees soared straight to the sky. The salt of the ocean and the tang of seaweed drenched the air. She'd have been soaking up the atmosphere like a sea sponge if only she could get her mind off sex and on to enjoying the weekend platonically. She'd been working hard. She needed the relaxation.

Bullshit. You need a good slam-bam-thank-you-sir.
That'll *unwind you.*

Rory's fingers clenched the wheel. She was so hy-peralert that her skin was jumping off her bones.

Ever since Tucker had walked in on the drawing class she'd been percolating with anticipation of the weekend ahead of them. Having used up all her will-power to stay calm at the time under his painstaking pe-rusal, she'd been left with no defense against his charms as the drive progressed. By the time they reached the resort, she'd be ready to ride him through the lobby like a bucking bronco.

Good thing she'd packed condoms.

Tucker was sprawled in the passenger seat, soaking up the sun with his seat tilted back.

"You didn't like it when I teased you about enjoying the posing, so naturally I'm curious about why you do it if you *don't* like it," he said, sounding lazy, but deter-mined.

Rory gritted her teeth. She didn't want to tell him about her struggle to appreciate her body for its health and ability instead of fixating on ten or twenty extra pounds. Or how she'd downed half a bottle of Beau-jolais to loosen her inhibitions when her turn to model had come up in class. She'd seem like a mess of anx-ieties when she wanted to impress him with her con-fidence.

"Why I do it is none of your business." That sound-ed too abrupt, so she added, "Trust me, it's no big deal."

Tucker didn't take offense. He didn't give up, either. "Is your mother a nudist?"

"She tells tales about the commune, but no. Although I don't look too closely when she's hot-tubbing with a boyfriend."

Tucker chuckled, fell into a long silence, then made one last stab. "I just didn't figure you for that type."

"There's a type?"

"Sure. A type I like. Uninhibited."

An easy lay with no expectations, she silently corrected, forgetting that she'd told herself not to underestimate him again.

"Then I've gone up in your esteem because you saw my nipples? That's ridiculous."

"They were worthy nipples."

They were hard as bullets. Every time a tight turn came up and she cranked the wheel, one of her arms would brush her breasts, sending a thrill shooting through her.

Don't think about that. "I can't believe we're having this conversation."

Tucker stretched. "What would you like to talk about?"

"Anything else!"

"Tell me about yourself."

"So you can look for signs of what turned me into a nudist?"

"No, I'm interested. Truly. We'll get back to why you take your clothes off later."

In their suite, in private, within proximity of a bed. Good Lord, Rory thought. The subject wasn't going away. She let up on the gas a bit and squirmed deeper into the car seat, warning herself not to run them off the road before they got there.

Tucker continued. "You said the other day that you used to be different, and that was why I didn't remember you from the party. What did that mean?"

"I was in my 'crunchy granola' phase."

"Ah, I see." All of Northern California was a hot spot for creatures of alternative habit.

"My hair was to my waist and my clothing was made of natural hand-loomed fibers. I wore glasses. I weighed—" She swallowed. "I weighed thirty pounds more than I do now. Stress eating—I hated my job. It's not that I was in really bad shape, because I liked to go on long hikes in the hills with my dog, but I was sort of soft and…lumpy."

She paused, but he didn't say anything. "Do you remember me now?"

"Maybe. Vaguely."

Oh, yeah, she'd made quite the impression.

"Hold on." He sat forward and lifted his sunglasses to squint at her. "I'm trying to picture this. What kind of dog?"

"Golden Retriever. His name was Maxwell. I got him when I was fifteen, but he's gone now." She smiled fondly, remembering her old pal Maxie up in doggy heaven. "Now I have two cats. They're easier to take care of with my busy schedule. Do you have pets?"

"Too much hassle. But I like dogs. Everyone in my family has at least one pet, to add to the general chaos. My brother Sam's family has a Golden named Chuckie Doll."

"What?" She laughed loudly when he explained how their teenage son had named the poor dog. "A movie name. I approve." She was starting to want to meet his family. He talked about them with such affection.

They continued driving. Rory pointed to the sea stack formations and Tucker leaned closer, craning his neck to see, saying, "Like a Zen rock garden in the ocean." They appreciated the view in silence for a moment, then his gaze shifted to her face. "What made you change since the wedding party?"

His shoulder nudged against her arm as he sat back again. She took a deep breath. "Everyone changes."

"I don't. I'm still the same guy I was back then."

So she'd been correct to believe that he had a Peter Pan complex.

"All right, if you insist," she said grimly. "*Most* people evolve. I had been doing social work after my graduation, along with Maureen Baxter. Raised the way I was, I'd naturally grown to believe that helping others was the career for me. But it turned out to be too stressful and depressing. I got way too emotionally involved with clients, which led to a fast burnout." She stretched her neck. "Mikki works within the system, but she can handle the load better than me. She's caring, but tough. I'm just too—"

"Soft," he put in.

"Yep."

"But not lumpy."

She cleared her throat. A gym membership and a regular pilates class had smoothed out her lumps, but she wasn't one of those girls who bounced around in thong leotards, comparing heart rates and Step Climber miles.

He wore a thoughtful expression, one that gave her goose bumps as she wondered what was on his mind. "So you opened Lavender Field instead," he said.

"Yes. Making bread was always a soothing activity for me." But certainly not a sexy occupation like lingerie model, which was probably what Tucker looked for in a woman.

As if she cared about meeting his desires.

Well, not *too* much.

"Emma and I used to make the household's bread for the week every Saturday morning. When my job got so stressful, I turned to kneading dough. Soon I was giving bread and rolls to anyone who'd take them. Then a guy I knew with a restaurant asked if I'd be his supplier, and before I knew it, I'd signed a lease for the first store."

"Then you're saying it was success that changed Rory Constable?"

She smiled at his movie title allusion. "Hmm, maybe. That and not being able to zip up my favorite pair of jeans." She glanced at his nicely fitted ones. Rather too fitted. She could tell he dressed to the left and that his package was more than nice. "You've never had that problem."

"Not yet. But I have the same physique as my dad and he's got a paunch now. When I start getting pudgy around the middle, I switch to light beer."

She shook her head. "Men. It's so easy for you. I gain if I even *look* at our pastry display."

"Exercise is the key. I stay active." Tucker's brows rose. "One way or the other."

Oh, boy. She could guess what he meant by *that.* "Um, this resort we're going to has many activities—golf, tennis, surfing, deep-sea fishing, horseback riding." She sounded like a travel brochure. "I haven't ridden in years."

"Then we should try that. Riding. Do you like to go fast?"

"Galloping?" Without a heavy-duty sports bra, she'd give herself a black eye. "I'm not sure I'm a good enough rider to be galloping."

"Be bold. We'll do it on the beach, in the surf. You just need to relax, find the rhythm and go with it. You'll love the adrenaline rush."

She gazed out over the ocean to the glow at the horizon, considering what type of ride he was talking about. "You can go for speed on your own. I'm more of a spa girl."

"Saunas and hot-stone massages? That sounds good to me."

Too good. She remembered what she'd said when Mikki had first told her about the raffle's grand prize. *A naked weekend with a stranger.* Tucker was no longer a stranger, but she still had qualms about getting naked with him.

Too hot. The long rays of the sun glanced off the windshield and she realized she was perspiring, even with the wind whipping against her face. She took one hand off the wheel and pushed the hood of her jacket off the back of her neck.

Tucker looked at her, his gaze dropping, then lingering on her chest. "You're wearing the necklace from the key party," he said, surprised. "How come?"

She glanced down. The suitcase locket had come untucked from the neckline of her tank top. "I don't know. I guess I just like it."

He reached over, holding the charm out for examination. Her breath caught at the heat of his skin.

His knuckles grazed her as the charm dropped between her breasts. "Damn, I don't have the key," he said, leaning back again and breaking the magnetic force between them.

Still prickling, she wet her lips. "What a shame."

"I don't know where it went. Do you think that's a sign?"

"A sign of what?"

"That we're not meant to be together."

She straightened her elbows. The key to the locket was in her purse. He'd left it in the suitcase locket on the night of party.

But he didn't have to know that—not until she'd made up her mind about him. "I guess we'll have to wait and see how the weekend goes."

He frowned. "If the weekend goes, it's already too late."

Then he was absolutely serious about this weekend being a one-shot deal. Rory's optimism, her hope that they might have something special, grew heavy. Her stomach got a sinking feeling, familiar from all the times she'd been let down by a man after getting her hopes up. But she fixed her shoulders and pushed the negative energy aside.

The way the day had worked out so far, with Tucker walking in on her posing for the art class and turning what might have been a humiliating moment into an interlude of heat and fire, made her think that their union was meant to be.

Even if it was only for the weekend.

8

"THIS PLACE is incredible," Rory said, walking around the spacious living room while Tucker tipped the bellman. The decor was beachy deluxe, with oversize armchairs made of woven water hyacinth, potted palms against pale aqua walls, and dark shining mahogany floors beneath the sisal rugs.

Instead of a suite in the main part of the hotel, they'd been given one of the luxury cottages that dotted the grounds. The bellman had pointed out the amenities, including a pergola draped in wisteria dripping with purple blossoms, a flagstone patio bordered by a low rock wall and the row of cypress and bushy pines that ensured the spa tub and small pool retained complete privacy.

They also had a bedroom balcony overlooking the ocean. Rory walked through the open French doors, drawn to the view. Beyond the green sweep of the resort grounds was the ocean. Gentle swells rolled toward shore, burnished like satin in the fading light. From nearby gardens, the scents of jasmine, honeysuckle and eucalyptus permeated the air.

Tucker joined her. "Maureen really went all out."

Rory breathed deeply. "Mmm-hmm. I'm in awe. I've definitely stopped being peeved that you switched keys with that guy at the party."

Tucker's hand caressed her bare arm. She'd dropped her jacket inside and was wearing only the flimsy tank top that felt like no barrier at all against her flushed skin.

"I didn't realize you were still peeved," he said.

She laughed lightly. "Oh, I'm not. That was a little kick to the ego, but I got over it quickly."

"His loss."

"For sure. If he could see this cottage…"

"No. If he could see *you*."

She smiled, nudging into Tucker's hand with her shoulder. "You're sweet."

"Nah, I'm selfish. I'm softening you up for when I make my big move."

His tone had been teasing, but his gaze was direct. She looked into his eyes for a couple of seconds, hoping for a kiss, ready for a kiss, *hungry* for a kiss.

Tucker made her wait.

His gaze moved across her features and for an instant she wished she'd gone into the bathroom to repair her makeup instead of only oohing over the whirlpool tub. But he wasn't concerned with melted mascara. He was looking at her lips.

They burned with anticipation.

"Lick them for me," he murmured.

Strands of hair had drifted across her face. She turned her face toward the ocean to blow them away, tilting her chin into the wind and closing her eyes as she slid her tongue between her lips. She rolled them against each other, slowly letting her bottom lip pout, wet and full.

"You're so sexy." Tucker put his hand on her cheek. "I have to kiss you."

Her lashes fluttered halfway open. "Don't hold back on my account."

He nuzzled her first, nipping at her mouth until she opened for him with a soft sigh. At that, he took hold of her hands and pressed closer. She met him, arching into the kiss with her chin tilted high and her breasts pushed against his chest.

The kiss became firm, even possessive. The anticipation she'd been feeling for hours burst into pleasure, making her body light up like fireworks. She wanted to run her hands over the hard muscles in his arms and shoulders, but he wouldn't let go, gripping her tightly as he applied his mouth, then his hot, velvet tongue, to the job of driving her mad with passion.

It was a very short trip.

Mmm, she wanted more. He seemed to be focused only on the kiss, while she was going up in flames all over her body. Her nipples pulled into tight buds, begging for the warm, wet relief of his mouth. A white-hot core of heat was centered between her thighs and she felt herself ripening, swelling, liquefying.

Tucker dragged in a long breath. A loud rumble came from his lower regions.

She could only think of the hard arousal that pressed against her butterfly-filled belly, until he said, "Sorry. I'm starved."

Of course. His stomach had growled. She smothered her giggle at her slow-witted reaction.

Tucker stepped back, bringing their knotted hands up to hold them against his chest. "Maybe," he said in between kisses, "we should do this for dessert instead."

She was loathe to stop, but he'd pulled his mouth away. His eyes were that luminous underwater-green again, gazing at her with a tenderness lit by desire, and she had to turn her face toward the ocean to gather her thoughts. Thankfully, a wind rose up off the waves and cooled her cheeks. She inhaled, and slowly the bracing salt air cleared her head.

Experimentally she moved her tongue around in her mouth, then made a harrumph sound in her throat. Seemed to be in working order.

She nodded. "Y-yes, it's better not to get carried away so soon."

Men were driven by their basic instincts and needs. Although sex was supposed to come before hunger, at least in this situation, they *had* traveled straight through without stopping for a meal. She was hungry, too.

"Let's go to dinner," she said, with only a brief glance of regret at the sweeping view. So much for romance. "But I really need a shower first. Can you get something from the minibar to stave you over?"

Tucker made a move to go inside. "That stuff costs a fortune."

She followed, still holding his hand. "I'll pay any extra charges we incur."

He gave her a P.O.'ed look. "Don't even think about it."

She squeezed his fingers. "But it gives me pleasure to share my good fortune now that my stores are doing so well—"

"That's great." He moved away into the other room, leaving her to stare at the bed draped in sheer curtains. She rubbed her damp palms against her thighs.

"But I'm not one of your charity cases," he added. "I do okay."

She leaned in the connecting archway. "I'm sure you do. I didn't mean to imply otherwise."

"So you know, I'm not particularly well-off, either. Just a regular blue-collar guy. I probably would never come to a place this nice for a vacation." He opened the miniature refrigerator tucked under the granite surface of the living room's wet bar and stared broodingly at the contents. "Five dollars for a bag of peanuts."

"There were a few munchies left in the cooler in the car."

"I'll manage. You go take your shower." Tucker's eyebrows shot up as he ripped into the bag of peanuts. "Unless you'd rather hop into the outdoor spa?"

She hovered. "I thought you were starving."

"We could get room service. That's included in our prize package."

The idea was tempting, except now that she was thinking again, she preferred to take her time. Spending the weekend with him so soon was already pushing her past her comfort zone.

The trip to Mendocino had flown by, in no small part thanks to his company. While it wasn't easy to be sensible when she was still rife with arousal, she recognized that with every moment they spent together, she was liking him more as a person, aside from their instant attraction.

But she wasn't ready to make a decision. Not cold, like this.

Or hot, rather. Especially if he'd continued kissing her...

Rory shook her head. Hadn't she wanted to be overwhelmed by desire? Swept away, so that she could say she'd hadn't been able to stop herself?

For a woman who prided herself on making wise choices, that was a cop-out. Nope, no spontaneity for her. The only way to do this was to approach the decision with a level head and to be clear and precise about the parameters.

But she was so very unclear at the moment. A cold shower and a full dinner should bring her back to normal.

"Not this time," she called to Tucker about his room service suggestion. "I'd rather get out and see the dining room and the rest of the resort. I promise I'll be quick." She walked into the bedroom and flipped quickly through the bag she'd left unzipped on a luggage stand.

When she lifted out her two dress choices for the evening—tailored linen or a floaty chiffon that appealed to the old her—the stash of her sexiest lingerie was revealed.

Revealed was right. One glimpse and Tucker would know that any move he made would be welcomed with open thighs.

Quickly, she piled her shorts and T-shirts on top of the silk and lace.

Who was she fooling?

She *knew* what her decision would be.

"YOU WOULDN'T dare!"

"Sure I would." Tucker started to strip out of his shirt.

"Pffft." Rory blew a raspberry at him. "You do it clothed, or there's no point."

"Naked would be more fun."

"For who?"

"You, of course."

She hesitated, smiling to herself as she nibbled at the alcohol-soaked fruit kabob plunked in the coconut shell of her frozen piña colada. "What an ego." She sucked a rummy chunk of pineapple off the skewer. "The question was, Have you ever jumped into a pool wearing your clothes?"

"I've been pushed in."

She waved at him from the lounge chair. "Oh, everyone's been pushed in. Big whoop."

"What do I win if I jump fully clothed?"

"Shoes, too?"

"Shoes, too."

She considered. "You win the chance to strip for me."

"That's a reward?"

"Makes sense to me."

"I think it should be the other way around."

"That's negotiable." She swiped the skewer around

the inside of the hollowed-out coconut. Nothing but slush. "Can I have your Tequila Sunrise?"

After dinner, an elegant affair in the formal dining room, she and Tucker had strolled the grounds, holding hands and talking and laughing, as comfortable as friends, but with the heady anticipation of knowing that they were about to become so much more.

When they'd returned to their bungalow, they'd both been nervous, so she'd suggested they call room service to deliver a couple of drinks from the bar. They'd taken them out to the pool, but Tucker had soon abandoned his for a beer.

"You can have it," he said, balancing on the lip of the pool in his dress shoes as he lifted an imported beer to his mouth. "If I can have Liquid Sex."

Rory's head wasn't quite swimming yet, but she'd certainly dunked it in the deep end. "Is that a drink or a porposition? I mean, a *prop*-o-sition."

Tucker sniggered. "I don't do poor positions. They're all very well executed and consumer rated A-plus."

With that, he set down the bottle, straightened with his hands over his head, and launched himself up and into the pool, performing a perfect jackknife dive.

Rory flung her legs off the side of the lounger and sat up. She stuck the tall icy glass between her knees to applaud. "Bravo!" she called when Tucker's head surfaced. "Most excellent! You even get a ten from the Russian judge."

He swam over to lean his arms against the coping. "I lost one of my shoes. Want to dive in and look for it with me?"

She took another slurp of the tequila and OJ mixture. "Gotta get into my swimsuit."

"Nah." He snaked his arm toward her feet, but she lifted them off the flagstones. He grabbed the leg of the lounge chair instead and began dragging it toward the pool with an ear-splitting screech of metal against stone.

Rory peered at him. "What the howdy-hey are you doing?"

"You've never been in a pool with your clothes on, have you? Not even pushed in. Tell the truth now."

She held her drink aloft in one hand and gripped the arm of the lightweight chair with the other as he inched the low end forward so it hung over the water. "That's an experience I'd rather not experience."

"C'mon, sweetheart," he taunted. "Live a little."

And he thrust up from the water, pushing his elbows down on the footrest of the chair.

It tilted. Rory shrieked. "Stop!"

He dipped back into the pool, holding her steady. "I'll give you ten seconds to jump."

She leaned over to put the drink on the stones, then sat heavily upright, her arms crossed. "I'm not moving."

"Ten."

"Not in my shoes. They're Coach, they match my bag."

"Nine, eight, seven."

"You're going too fast!"

"Six, five, four-three-two-one."

She was halfway out of the chair when he lunged

up out of the water like a porpoise, using all his weight to press down on the end of the chair and flip her into the pool.

With a scream—more of disbelief than outrage—she hurtled into the aqua water, face-first and making a huge splash. The plunge sent her toward the bottom of the pool, but before she could get her bearing and swim to the surface, Tucker was behind her, winding his arms around her waist.

She relaxed against him, letting her arms and legs float as he kicked them to the surface.

They popped up out of the water. Sputtering, she broke away from him, turning as she pushed her hair out of her face. "Tucker! You are such a brat."

His arms were outspread as he calmly treaded water beside her. "That's what my family says."

She bobbed. "Someone needs to take you in hand."

A dastardly glint shone in his eyes. "You offering?"

Her heart was already racing from the dunk in the pool, but it managed to pick up a few beats. "I'll give you the back of my hand."

"I want the front." He reached through the water to find and kiss her palm. A frisson went up her arm when instead of letting go his tongue continued to lick at her wet skin. He kissed her wrist, sucked at the inside of her elbow. He reached around her waist.

In a swirl of ripples, they came together. "*And* I want the back," he said, putting both hands on her derriere and pulling her snugly up against him.

She was transfixed.

"'N everything in the middle," he muttered into her

neck, kissing a path from her throat to the underside of her jaw.

Her fingers plunged into his wet hair, holding it by the roots as she tipped his head back and planted an unapologetically carnal kiss on him, sick and tired of holding back. As soon as she'd made her point, she let him go with a wrenching motion and sucked air through her nostrils. "You got me. All weekend, the way you wanted."

"You've got to want it, too," he said.

She moved beneath his searching hands, kicking her feet, rolling her hips. "It seems that I do."

"Seems that way," he said with a chuckle as he found the hard knot of one of her nipples. He played it with his fingers, the sensations somehow heightened by the fact that she couldn't see what he was doing.

Above the waterline, the bare skin of her arms and face, neck and shoulders prickled in the cool night air. Below, silken, heated water flowed over her in delicious contrast. He'd managed to loosen her dress so it floated around her like seaweed, as diaphanous as a mermaid's garment. The deep décolletage of her bra gave him easy access, and he plucked and strummed at her distended nipples, sometimes dipping his fingers inside her bra, sometimes not, then sinking below the surface and using his mouth before withdrawing to gasp for air. Always there was a caress, continuously moving, continuously teasing, until she gave up any pretense and let herself fall back, her face aimed at the sky.

She floated, his hand at her back. Her breasts crested the water and he laved them with broad swipes of his tongue, lapping her like the water as they drifted slowly toward the pool's edge.

The night had deepened. Desire hummed inside her; it throbbed at her lips, her fingertips, at her core. Between the night sky dotted by stars and the glistening dark water and the steady rhythm of the ocean, she couldn't tell if she floated or flew.

Tucker steadied them with a hand on the coping. "Do you want to get out?"

Reluctant, but knowing no perfect moment was forever, she lifted her head and shook the water from her ears. "You first."

With an enviable athleticism, he levered himself from the pool in one clean motion and stood dripping in his soaked clothing: a white button-down shirt gone almost sheer and clinging to every ripple in his abdomen, midnight-blue dress pants glued to his thighs and the bulge beneath his fly.

The very prominent bulge. Or so it seemed to Rory, gazing up at him from the water.

He kicked off a lone shoe and peeled out of his sodden socks, then leaned down to her and offered his hand. She looked for the steps, but they were on the other side, miles away in her distorted perception.

She gave him her hand and heaved up out of the water, the strength of his pull landing her on her feet. Uneasily, she plucked at her dress, which seemed to be unzipped and barely staying up, but still managed to cover her, in a manner of speaking. The flowered chiffon would be practically transparent, with her silk-and-lace lingerie leaving little to Tucker's imagination.

Not that he needed to imagine, she realized. Tucker had already seen her naked.

She wavered, pressing a hand over her mouth as she blinked at the lounge chair canted nearby. Five minutes ago…ten minutes…how much time had passed? Could have been an hour, for all she was aware. When Tucker touched her, time stopped.

And pleasure began.

Don't be a dweeb, she told herself, then asked, "What do we do now?" Inane, but it was something to say.

"We get out of these wet clothes and into the spa." The tub bubbled merrily only steps away, raised one level above the pool. He walked toward it, unbuttoning his shirt as he went. It dropped with a wet plop on the flagstones.

"Sounds like I'm gonna find out about that Liquid Sex."

"It's a drink. Tequila and rum and something else. Maybe whipped cream, too."

"Let's order one." She picked up the drink she'd abandoned and took a sip from the straw before following him. Two steps and she stopped to frown at her feet. "My shoes are wet."

Brilliant deduction.

"C'mere," he said.

Her eyes narrowed. Tucker's pants had joined his shirt. He was stripped to his skivvies, completely unabashed that she could see the outline of his semierect penis through the white cotton briefs.

Semierect? I can do something about that.

She moved toward him, swaying on her ridiculously steep heels as she sucked noisily on the curly straw. The remaining ice rattled. She shook the glass, wondering why the stones were tilting.

"You've had enough of this," he said, taking the empty glass from her.

With a sound of protest and a distinct squelch, she planted her butt beside his. She looked down at the sodden wrinkled mess crisscrossing her abdomen. "What am I wearing?" She scraped at the dress.

He peeled it off, then removed her shoes, leaving her clad only in her underwear—rose-colored satin and lace, bikinis and bra, both skimpier than she normally wore. Unfortunately, that fact was beginning to clear her head.

With more haste than grace, she swung her legs over the side of the spa and sank beneath the bubbling froth. "Ahh-hh. Come on in. Water's fine."

"In my shorts?"

She flung her head back to examine him with one eye squinted shut. "I give up. What's in your shorts?"

"One guess." He shrugged and climbed into the tub.

She bit back a silly response, aware that her alcohol high was making her giddy. She'd rather impress him with her sexy, sophisticated cool, but it was probably too late for that. "I'm afraid I can't say."

"Are your faculties impaired?"

"They might be." She moved through the water to his side of the tub. "I was always better at blindfolded guessing games. You know, the kind where you try to identify things with your fingers?" She brushed against his chest. "I'd be willing, if only my faculties weren't impaired."

"We can play another kind of game, but you'll have to concentrate."

Not easy when there was his gorgeous tanned chest to stare at. "I can try."

He rose out of the hot tub and reached toward the flat arc of lawn bordered by pebbles. She stared happily at his magnificent rear end, the taut buns clearly outlined in drenched white cotton. Goodness gracious, but she was a lucky girl, winning this weekend getaway with the man of her fantasies.

Her hand reached for the suitcase charm dangling around her neck. Her lucky charm. She was never letting go of it.

"Here you are," Tucker said, resettling himself while holding something out to her.

She had to put both hands out to take his offering. Pebbles. Walnut-size pebbles. "Uh, thanks."

"That's your stake."

"My stake?"

"For playing I Never. Do you know the game?"

"I don't think so." She followed his lead and made a small pile of the pebbles on the wet pavers that ringed the tub.

"It's easy enough. I'll start and you'll soon get the drift." He shook a couple of the pebbles in a lightly knotted fist. "I've never drunk an entire Tequila Sunrise." He grinned. "Now you owe me a stone."

"Beg your pardon?"

"You *have* drunk a Tequila Sunrise, so you lose."

"Ah," she said, getting it. He reached for her little pile of pebbles and she slapped his hand away. "Not so fast."

"You lose. You just drank—"

"But not an *entire* one. You ordered it. You had a sip, remember?" She hooted at the flummoxed expression. "Gotcha."

He conceded the point. "Okay, you're right. On a technicality."

"Do I get a pebble?"

"Only on your own turn."

"Lemme think, then. I have to concentrate." She closed her eyes to steady her senses. "Okay, I've got one." She smiled at him. "I've never jumped into a pool with my clothes on."

He was momentarily speechless. Then he handed her one of his pebbles. "Are you sure you haven't played this game before?"

"Nope. But I'm a quick learner." And a woman of inadequate experience. Who knew that would finally be to her benefit?

"Wait a minute. What about tonight? You're wringing wet."

Yeah, and he didn't know nothin' yet. "Doesn't count. You *pulled* me in."

He groaned. "Another technicality."

She dropped his pebble onto her pile. "Your turn."

With a Cheshire-cat grin, he sat back in the tub, stretching his arms out along the sides with a satisfied air. "I've never posed nude for an art class."

"Cheap one. But you got me." She lobbed a pebble

at him. He didn't react quick enough and it skidded off the pavers into the bubbling water.

He searched, his chin dipping below the surface. "Can't find it."

"I'll look." She dunked her head and was instantly hit by a blast from the jets. Feeling along the bottom of the tub, she encountered Tucker's legs, then the pebble. It went into her cleavage and with her hands on his thighs, she surfaced right in front of him. She shook droplets from her face and dripping hair. "Got it."

"I can feel your hands," he said, widening his thighs beneath her sliding caress so she fit between them, "and you're not holding a rock."

She climbed into his lap instead, allowing her palm to brush the front of his briefs once more. Rock-hard. She reached for another feel. "You underestimate yourself."

Because they were right there in front of him, he was looking at her breasts, bursting out of the lacy bra cups. "Your breasts have that effect on me."

She looked down and giggled. "Are there two pebbles in my bra, or am I just happy to meet you?"

He framed her with his hands, squeezing so her cleavage deepened even more. "I don't see any actual *pebbles*…" His lower half shifted. "But you are coming out of this flimsy contraption."

"Soon, I hope."

Tucker had hooked a finger in her bra to undo the front fastenings when he found the pebble. He fished it out and tossed it over his shoulder. It skittered into the darkness.

"Are we done playing?" she asked.

"I think it's your turn."

"Hmm." She considered for all of two seconds before blurting the most provocative suggestion she'd ever dared give a man. "I've never had my nipples sucked in a hot tub."

9

MAN. SHE WAS REALLY going for it. Unless this wasn't about the game and she was thinking only of taking her pleasure. If so, he was into that.

Still, Tucker's eyes narrowed. He couldn't let her bamboozle him. "The rule of the game is, you have to tell the truth."

Rory hung her head. "What I said…" Her voice was small. Strings of wet hair obscured her face. "Sad, but true."

"Then I owe you a pebble."

"Oh. So you *have* had yours sucked?" Instantly she was spunky again, tossing her hair as she scoffed at herself. "What am I saying? Of course you have."

Uh-oh. Delicate territory. "I've been in a few hot tubs."

"And more than a few willing ladies, I suspect," she replied in the wry tone she used whenever she was feeling less than confident. If she hadn't been sitting in his lap, pressing her hot sex against his engorged cock, he might have believed she was having doubts about becoming another pebble in his collection.

"The better question is how come *you* haven't?"

She shrugged, idly tracing a design on his chest. "Lack of opportunity."

"But you were engaged. You must have been in a few hot tubs with the guy."

Her body gave a jolt that raised her a couple of inches off his lap. He thought she might have wanted to flee, but she was too stricken to move far. "How do you know about my long-lost fiancé? That was more than ten years ago."

"I asked Nolan," he said.

"Then you must also know that I was ditched at the altar." Her brittle laugh was meant to show how little that mattered, but he wasn't buying that one, either. She held herself stiffly. "Too bad for me, huh? The hot-tub-nipple-sucking was scheduled for the honeymoon."

Tuck made sympathetic sounds as he caressed her arms, her shoulders, soothing her as he urged her back down. "He only said that the marriage was called off."

In truth, Nolan had spilled more than that, telling the story of how Rory's fiancé had taken off with another woman only days before the wedding, because he'd fallen in love at first sight, and then had the gall to expect Rory to be understanding.

"That's fairly accurate. Brad and I didn't actually make it to the altar, but close enough."

"Nolan and I decided that the man was a jerkwad of the highest order. You're better off without him."

"I came to that conclusion myself." Her head tilted to one side and she blinked at him, a genuine smile teasing at her pouted lips. "Still, I should get a pebble for being a jilted bride, don't you think?"

He chuckled. "I know I've never been one."

She nestled in closer, letting her breasts pillow on his chest. "Mmm," she hummed into his ear. "You've probably never even come close."

Land mine territory. He gripped her hips so that she wouldn't explode without him. "Nope."

But she remained relaxed. With a lazy stretch, she rested her arms on his shoulders. "I should be careful around you, then."

"Why? You think I'm gonna break your heart?"

"Hell, no. I just don't want you falling in love with *me* and getting all mushy-gushy. This weekend isn't for that."

Although he knew she was teasing with him to avoid a serious topic, he couldn't stop himself from asking, "Who says I've never been in love?"

"Nobody. But I can tell."

He let that one go, because he couldn't remember, offhand, if he'd ever really loved any of the women he'd dated, even the ones who'd lasted longer than a month. "What about you? Any close calls since the jerkwad?"

"Scads of them."

"But none that got you into a hot tub?"

"I don't look good as a prune."

He pressed his fingers into the firm flesh of her ass. The bikini panties were riding low. Two tugs and he'd have her naked and sumptuous. Two tugs of his *mouth* and she'd be begging to give back a pebble.

She sighed, straightening again. "Okay, that was evasive. I'm not good at lying. The truth is there haven't been a lot of men. I like to think I'm careful about who

I get involved with, but Lauren and Mikki say I'm just a coward."

"That's not what I see."

"You're looking at my breasts."

"Yeah. So? If you were a coward, I wouldn't be."

She wiggled. "That's right. I'm here. Do with me what you will before your, uh, thighs go numb."

"There's no danger of that." He ran his hands along her smooth wet back. "I'm feeling you with every inch of my body."

"You always say the right thing. Such a glib tongue."

"The better to suck you with."

She rose a little and slowly undid her bra. The tiny hooks at the front popped apart one by one. "I have never stripped outdoors, unless you count the time I went into a Navajo sweat lodge."

"Technically…" he said, but his voice gave way when her remaining hook did the same and her breasts spilled out, fulfilling every fantasy he'd had for this weekend, including the hundred or so he'd conjured up on the drive north when he'd been sure she would absently reach over and mistake his constant arousal for the stick shift. He hadn't been this hard for so long since he was eighteen.

With other women, he wouldn't have waited.

But Rory was worth every painful, painstaking minute.

"I've never wanted a woman this bad," he said.

"I've never wanted a man…"

"Then we have a draw."

"Forget the game," she whispered, her lips barely

moving. They looked so ripe he couldn't decide what to kiss first.

"Take this," she said, reading his mind. Her hands were on her breast, trying to insert the nipple into his mouth.

"Wait. You're all wet." He lapped the beaded droplet with his tongue several times, making her nipple bobble.

She took in a sharp breath.

"This one, too," he said, switching sides.

A guttural moan. "Please…"

He licked a careful circle all around the pebbled flesh before closing his mouth over the rigid nub at the center. Still, he didn't suck. He held her between his lips and kept his tongue flickering until she was squirming, urging him on with her hips, her biting grip, her desperate voice. "Tuck, *please.*"

"Mumph." His mouth opened wide to take her in. Instinct raged and he sucked hard, wanting more of her soft body, more of her sweet surrender. Before he was through, she'd have abandoned all her proprieties and become a wild, wanton, totally willing woman.

If she wasn't already.

"Yesss," she hissed, rocking against him. Gentle hands cradled the back of his head, pressing more firmly when he went for the other nipple. "That's just right. Don't stop, Tucker. Don't stop."

No chance of that. He lost himself in her, shifting one from one breast to the other, tasting every inch of the bountiful flesh, moving up to her mouth for minutes at a time, but never relinquishing her ultrasensitive nipples. She was beautifully responsive to each tug and tweak, riding his lap like a wave. Rising, coasting, dropping with a deep sigh. Always ready for the next swell as the pleasure mounted.

She was up on her knees, arms braced on the edge of the hot tub, her breasts filling his face, when he felt her give a quick, sharp inhale. A shudder went through her. Her hips made hunching movements against his ribs and he took firm hold of her ass, sucking deeply on the nipple in his mouth.

She whimpered, "Oh-hh…no…I'm…"

"Yes," he mumbled.

"I really can't," she said, though she was.

He let go of her breasts and wrapped both hands around her hips. Although he was dying to get his fingers inside her, to stroke her throbbing clit, he didn't have to. She was coming. Her body shook, then stiffened, her voice rising to the stars.

And she collapsed.

He nuzzled in between her breasts. "That was beautiful."

She clung to him with her face pressed into his shoulder. "I'm so embarrassed. We didn't even—even—"

"There's time for that."

"But I'm spent." She moved off him, avoiding his eyes as she lifted a shaky hand to her damp, tangled hair. "I've *never*—"

She stopped and clamped her mouth shut.

Despite her disbelief, she'd also never looked more replete. Her face was calm, her cheeks flushed pink, her eyes darkly luminous in the low lighting.

"You've never what?" he prompted.

Her voice was soft, almost shy. "Come so easily. Without any, um, direct stimulation."

Hard to believe, given her responsiveness. "Then you haven't been with the right man."

"Obviously."

"Stick with me, kid," he teased, but his cocksure pride dropped a couple of notches as his brain clicked in and he remembered the boastful credo passed among his fellow construction workers: give a woman an orgasm and she'll be back, begging for more.

Did he want that?

Usually he'd be uneasy at the thought of a woman depending on him, even if it was only for orgasms. But this time, the answer was easy.

Did he want Rory wanting him?

You bet.

THEY SAT SILENTLY for several minutes, languishing in the hot bubbling water. At least, Rory was languishing. She was so relaxed her limbs felt like overstretched rubber bands. If Tucker's hand hadn't been clasped on the back of her neck, she might have slid below the surface, a dopey smile still plastered to her face.

The sky was midnight-blue, dotted with stars. She tilted her face toward them, letting her eyes close. Mmm. Tucker's fingers tunneled into her hair and gently kneaded her scalp.

She took a deep breath, vaguely aware that this made her breasts bob up to skim the waterline.

He groaned. She reached under water and put her

hand on his thigh, too lazy to slide her butt over and give him what he deserved. She petted the tense muscles bunched beneath her palm. "Let me take a few minutes to recover and I'll make you happy you waited."

"This isn't playschool. We don't have to take turns."

"No?" Every man she'd ever been with expected tit for tat.

Tat for tit might be more appropriate in this case, she decided with an inward grin.

Tucker slid a hand beneath her bottom. "I'm willing to give until it hurts."

Her eyes flew open. She shot him a surprised look as he lifted her from the tub in a gush of water, quickly laying her right there on the flagstones with her head in the strip of lush grass and her rear end on the rim of the spa. Her legs dangled in the water. Deftly, he parted them and rose up between her thighs with a leer and what might be called a spear from the feel of it, like some sort of erotic Neptune.

She found the strength to rise up on her elbows. "What are you doing?"

One his palms pressed against her abdomen while the other smoothed along the inside of her thigh. "Shh, Rory. Lie back and enjoy the ride."

"But I'm so—"

He'd caught his thumbs in her underpants and dragged them down.

She gulped as the cool night air wafted across her red-hot vulva. "Exposed."

His voice hummed with appreciation. "You have nothing to worry about. No one can see but me."

Her head lifted. "You think that doesn't worry me?"

"It shouldn't. You're the sexiest sight I've seen since those two hot volleyball chicks wore their itty-bitty bikini bottoms in the Olympics."

"Oh, well, if *that's* the case," she drawled with a casual shrug. Part of her wondered if the compliments were only more of his silver-tongued charm, but he seemed sincere. Anyway, arguing would be futile when it was so much easier to enjoy the moment for what it was.

With a nervous laugh, she dropped her head down, covering her eyes with her hands. Wings fluttered in her stomach when his hand grazed across her inflamed sex, but she was still too weak and pliant to put up even the most token resistance. Besides, it wasn't as though she truly wanted to.

Tucker must have stood on the tub's seat because suddenly he loomed above her again. His hands went to her flattened breasts and pushed them together, making a line of deep cleavage that he planted with fiery kisses until he'd reached her throat.

He licked the hollow. "I thought you were ready to conk out, but your heart is racing."

"I'm perking up."

His thumbs swiped her taut nipples. "Yes, you certainly are."

She gave a small gasp at the stinging sensation.

"Too sensitive?"

"A little."

He kissed her. "I'll find something else to play with."

She didn't dare ask, but he wasted no time in making his intentions clear. While he licked and sucked his way back the way he'd come, his fingers were busy elsewhere. They danced between her thighs, teasingly nudged against her swollen labia, then retreated to stroke her backside or to comb through the small patch of hair before dipping into her again, each intimate touch sending another shock wave reverberating through her.

His tongue swirled into the shallow cup of her belly button. Even that was intense and erotic. But it was his touch that she fixated on, waiting breathlessly for him to reach the flashpoint of her desire. She needed that. Already. Again.

She needed *him*.

"It's okay," she said, pushing to her elbows. "I'm ready. You can—ah…you know."

He looked up, his expression as taunting as her fingers. "Tell me."

She did. Two words that left nothing to the imagination. No sense in being coy about it.

"I'll get there," he promised, "soon enough."

"But you must be hurting by now. I know I am."

He smiled tightly. "Let me take this trip my way. The slow scenic route."

"Whatever you like. But don't say I didn't offer."

His hot-as-sin gaze went directly to her exposed genitals. "Darling, there's no missing your open invitation."

Self-consciousness washed through her and she tried to close her legs, but he wasn't letting her. With a small splash, he slid lower in the spa, keeping his shoulders wedged between her thighs as he picked them up in his hands and levered her open, so open there was nothing she could do but give in with a grateful groan as he put his mouth to her and drove his tongue deep. Several times, he stabbed in and out, in and out, making her cry out, hips pumping.

"Not so fast," he murmured, withdrawing to apply his fingers and lips in a gentler exploration. The pace was an excruciating tease of advance and retreat, always slowing when her muscles tightened with the climactic tension. Her body was shaking, her mind gone blank to all but physical sensation, her clit too tender to be touched but too needy not to want to.

Finally he lapped at her, the same way he'd toyed with her nipples. She almost cried in relief. He drove a finger into her, his knuckles rubbing the rim of sensitive nerve endings as she rose into the raw pleasure, begging that this time he wouldn't stop. She couldn't take the torture—she had to explode.

As if he already knew her body's rhythms and needs, he flattened his tongue firmly in place, keeping her anchored as the leaping ecstasy sent her spinning. She bucked against his mouth as the spasms rocketed through her, but his hands were there, and his wide strong shoulders.

For once she gave herself up, never having felt so secure and accepted, so at ease with the vulnerability of her position. The resulting climax was incredible and intense, but the sweetest release she'd ever been given. She knew she was okay with Tucker, even when she lost control of her rational self and drifted away into an exhausted state of bliss.

RORY DIDN'T WAKE until morning. She found herself sprawled in bed, completely nude but draped in a sheet, every inch of her body replete and relaxed.

A few minutes passed before she remembered the night before. Much of it was hazy, especially after the second mind-blowing climax. How had she landed in bed? Had they made love?

She lifted her head. "Tucker?"

No answer but the pounding water of the shower.

Grateful for the time alone to gain her senses, she rolled over onto her back and felt along her body for clues. Her nipples were tender to the touch. The muscles in her thighs and buttocks twinged when she flexed. Pleasantly used, not dissimilar to the feeling she had after a bike ride or a hike.

She sat up, stretching her legs this way and that before she pulled them up to her chest in a hug. No signs of love bites or bruises. Tucker had been gentle when she'd needed to slow down and fierce when she'd wanted it hard.

And all of their erotic adventures had been one-sided.

Unless she'd totally passed out and couldn't remember…but no. She'd be able to tell. He'd put her to bed, unboffed but not unloved.

The man was working his way into her heart.

"Hey, sleepyhead." He walked into the room, rubbing a towel over his wet hair. A second towel was slung low around his hips, making her mouth go dry.

She worked up some spit. "What's going on?"

"Plenty. I've made plans for the day."

"Such as…?"

"Breakfast should be delivered any minute. Afterward we're hitting the beach. Horseback riding and a picnic follow, then when we get back I've scheduled a few hours at the spa for you—"

"Alone?"

"Do you want me to come along?"

A naked weekend required a naked man. "If you'd like to."

"I'll make a call." There was a knock at the sitting room door and Tucker went to answer it, saying over his shoulder, "We'll finish up with a romantic dinner on the hotel terrace overlooking the ocean, and then…"

He didn't finish the sentence, but she could imagine. Woo, could she ever!

While he was busy with the room service attendant, she jumped off the bed and ran for a robe. A mirror check revealed better news than she'd expected. Yes, her hair was a tangled mess and her eye makeup was smudged, but her eyes were shining, her skin was fresh and practically dewy. There was definitely a sensually satisfied look about her.

"After dinner, there's a blues singer who performs in the resort lounge, or we can drive into town." Tucker came back into the room, dropped his towel and bent over the duffel he'd pulled out of the armoire. "Tomorrow, I'd thought we tour Mendocino. You can scour the shops and I'll find something to amuse me. Maybe we can take a bike ride along the cliffs, or go sailing. Whatever you'd like."

During all of this, he was putting on his clothes.

Stepping into briefs and shorts, yanking a polo shirt over his head, completely unconcerned that she hovered in the doorway to the bath, watching the lovely shift and flex of his bronzed muscles and wishing that his penis hadn't been tucked away so quickly.

The shirt dropped over his flat washboard stomach and finally he looked at her, concerned about her silence. "Is that all right?"

"It's perfect. Well, almost." She raked a hand through her hair, frowning slightly.

"Got a headache? Those two drinks really did you in last night."

"Did you have to carry me to bed?"

"You were able to walk, but you seemed pretty bleary."

She winced. "I vaguely remember. But I'm fine now. Great, in fact. But I, uh, don't believe it was the alcohol alone that knocked me out."

"You're saying it was…?"

"You."

He grinned. "I like to show a girl a good time."

The understatement made her laugh in disbelief. "You certainly accomplished your goal." She paused, aware of the low hum of sexual desire building inside her, aiming toward the peak she'd reached the night before. Maybe, incredibly, beyond that point once she knew what it was like to have him thrusting inside her.

"I have only one question about this schedule of yours," she said.

"Yeah?"

"When do we make love?"

10

"AHH-HH."

"You like it?" Tucker said.

Rory closed her eyes and luxuriated in the sensation. "Oo-ooh, yess-ss."

"Me, too. But it's hot in here. I didn't think it'd be so hot."

"The heat's what makes it good. I think my bones are melting. Mmm-hmm."

He chuckled. "If I didn't know better, I'd say you sound like you're approaching climax."

Her lids popped open. "Tucker! Hush. There are attendants around."

"They left five minutes ago and they won't be back. You were too busy moaning to notice."

"I can't help it." She smiled. "I've never been in a mud bath before. It's wonderful for my sore muscles."

"Sore muscles, huh?" He winked from the adjacent rectangular stone tub, each one filled to the brim with a viscous brown mud. The surface of the goo shimmered and steamed, broken now and then by the thick bubbles that popped as they rose to the top.

"Sore from the horseback riding," she said. "And

from keeping up with you in general. You're as active as a teenager. Where do you get your never-ending supply of giddy-up-and-go?"

Sagely he rubbed a hand over his chin, giving himself a mud goatee. "It's pent-up sexual energy."

"Oh, I see." Rory tried to shift, but the mud was so heavy, movement required too much effort. "You should have taken me up on my offer this morning. For both our sakes. Then I could have spent the entire day lounging on a beach towel instead of bouncing from one activity to another."

"If I had, the schedule would have been blown to smithereens."

"The schedule." She sent him a disbelieving look.

"It's not that I'm into order, but if we'd had sex," he explained patiently, "it would have been an all-day affair. Once I get you into bed, you're not crawling out for hours. You'd have missed the massage and the mud baths."

She made a face. "To say nothing of Trigger."

"Hey. You weren't a bad rider. Didn't you enjoy it, at least a little?"

"Yeah, I did. You know I'm teasing." She'd been unsure about getting on the back of the horse—a placid paint actually called Perdita—so she'd made fun of herself. A protective defense mechanism. One earth-shaking experience with Tucker wasn't enough to change a lifetime of self-deprecating habit.

"The picnic was very nice," she added. "Did I remember to thank you?"

They'd driven a couple of miles to the stables,

mounted up and ridden the horses along the spectacular waterfront, with much splashing and joking. When they'd arrived at the resort's private beachfront, they'd found a picnic lunch awaiting them, delivered and arranged at Tucker's request. His forethought and caring had touched Rory's heart and they'd had a good long talk about everything under the sun, from California politics—they'd voted for different parties and had engaged in a rousing debate—to a battle of movie trivia. Tucker had even managed to stump her with an astonishing knowledge of Bela Lugosi movies. Turned out he was a creature-feature maven.

"Did *I* remember to thank *you?*" he countered. "You're good company, Rory."

"Likewise." From the start, she'd thought he was handsome, with a genial personality, but she hadn't expected to like him so much as a friend.

He sank lower in the tub so that even his shoulders were submerged. "We'll get along fine."

She blinked at the non sequitur. "What do you mean?"

"You know…afterward."

"Oh, yes." But she didn't like the implication. Apparently nothing had changed for him. Whereas the sexual experience had rocked *her* world to the core.

Get your feet under you, girl. Hot sex and a long talk on the beach do not a relationship make. Next time he sees you, it's going to be all "Hey, there, Rory. Didn't we have fun together once upon a time? Meet my new girlfriend. Her name is Tiffani and she's a swimsuit model."

The silence stretched. Mud bubbles blipped and burped. Steam trickled down the stone walls of the grotto style spa room. Aside from the double tubs, the only furnishings in the dark, enclosed space were a couple of simple wooden benches, a row of hooks for towels and robes and a large palm glistening with condensation.

"There *is* going to be an afterward, right?" Tucker ventured, sounding less certain.

She wasn't sure what he was asking. Did he want to know if they were still planning to have sex or was he negotiating the consequences?

"There's always an afterward," she said. *Usually uncomfortable*.

"Good," he said. "I guess."

Rory bit her lip. In her dating experience, it was never a good sign when the man she was with worried about dumping her before their date was over. If she had more pride and less craving, she'd give Tucker the heave-ho first.

Was it foolish or merely practical of her to want to have sex with him first? She needed this weekend. She *deserved* this weekend.

If only she could think of him as a temporary stud. A boy-toy.

But, no, she had to go and get to know him as *person*, dammit.

Rory dredged up an arm and started slapping handfuls of the warm mud on her face and throat. She didn't want Tucker to see her doubts. He'd probably have second thoughts if it seemed as though she was becoming attached. And she wasn't through with him yet.

"Hey, watch where you're slinging that muck," he said. "Ptooey."

"Sorry." She flung another scoop of the sticky stuff and a glob of it landed in his hair.

He struggled to sit up in the tub. "You aimed that one."

"Oh, did the overspray get you?" She blinked, catching a glimpse of the rim of mud around her eyes as it started to crust over.

"Overspray? That was a direct hit."

"It's good for your skin."

He snorted. "Is that why you look like the *Creature From the Black Lagoon?*"

She patted the mud's surface. "Directed by Jack Arnold, 1954."

"Starring?" He scooped up a handful and threatened her with it.

"Richard Carlson and Julia Adams."

The mud glopped onto his own head. "Never heard of them, so I'll have to take your word for that. But don't think I won't be checking it on the Internet when I get home."

She tilted her chin. "You do that."

He leaned partway out of his tub, his elbows on the ledge. "You know, your mouth looks really pink and juicy surrounded by all that mud."

She pushed through the muck to meet him. "You ever kissed a mud creature?"

"Mmm."

Her eyes widened. "Don't tell me. You *have.*"

"There was this crazy girl. She participated in a

mud-wrestling match one night at a bar and afterward…"

"I said not to tell me." Rory dangled her mud-caked arms over the side. "Is there anything you haven't done?"

His gaze touched on her bulging cleavage. "I can name at least one thing."

"Now I'm a thing?"

"A beautiful and desirable thing." He reached for her hand to pull her closer. "When the mud's washed off."

"Good to know Miss Crazy didn't leave you with a mud fetish."

"I'd rather taste you," he said just before his mouth met hers. She leaned into the kiss, eager despite her misgivings, the *I need this, I deserve this* refrain running through her head.

Tucker tasted of wine and the ocean and a little bit of mud. Or maybe that was her.

He suckled her tongue, then left her with a long, slow slurp. "Wanna get dirty with me?"

"I'm more into good, clean fun."

He heaved himself out of the sludgy tub. "Then let's hit the showers."

She gave him her hand and he helped her slither out of the clinging mud. She'd worn a conservative one-piece suit, but the immersion in head-to-toe, nook-to-cranny mud had the effect of making her look nude under its slick coating.

Tucker's baggy surf shorts were clinging, leaving very little to the imagination. The shiny layer of goo delineated every muscle. His pecs were prominent. His nipples looked like little brown beads. Thicker rivulets ran down his stomach, clotting in the hollows of his hipbones and the low-slung waistband of his shorts, which were dragged down by the weight of the muck. The shape of his penis was—

Rory blinked. *Well, let's just say there's no need for a tape measure.*

He studied her with equal interest. When he looked up and smiled, the white of his teeth was dazzling. "This mud is very revealing."

"That's what I was thinking."

"Are you as hot as I am?"

"Are we speaking literally or figuratively, or do you just have a very large ego?"

His brow creased, cracking the splotches of mud. "It's not fair to ask me multisyllabic questions when your headlights are on."

She rolled her eyes at his teasing, resisting the urge to put her hands over her breasts. "Are you one of those guys who has a million euphemisms for women's breasts? Hooters, honkers, bazookas and bazongas and all the rest?"

He took her hand and led her to the shower area, a cubicle seemingly chiseled out of stone. "Actually, no. But we can formally name them, if you'd prefer." He considered. "How about Thelma and Louise?"

"Not my favorite movie. I prefer happy endings."

"Franny and Zooey?" Shower heads dotted the enclosure. When he turned on the spigots, they were blasted with water from all directions.

She shot him a surprised look before ducking under a shower head. "You read J. D. Salinger?"

"Been known to. Wait—I've got it." He smoothed her hair back, scraping away handfuls of the mud. "Butch Cassidy and the Sundance Kid."

"Tucker…" She finished rinsing her face and turned to face him. "Why don't you just kiss me?"

"They die, too," he murmured, dipping toward her lips. "Butch and the Kid."

Rory felt certain that she'd rather suffer *la petit mort*. Fortunately, their kiss was heaven-on-earth and she didn't have to go anywhere except into Tucker's arms.

Still kissing, he cupped her breasts. "But these are very much alive."

"I'm tingling all over."

"Me, too."

"Could be from the massage or the mud, but I doubt it." She spread her hands over his chest, helping to wash away the streaks of mud. The blasting water had flattened his chest hair. Her fingertips followed the narrowing strip to a point well above his navel. She detoured and found the line again, where it disappeared into his waistband.

He was nibbling at her neck. Stroking her breasts. "Don't stop now," he said when she hesitated.

"Your suit's all muddy."

"So's yours."

She contemplated the dilemma. There was only one way to get really clean.

And really dirty.

"I'll strip if you strip," she said, her pulse rate picking up a few counts even though he'd already seen her naked.

"No deal." With a wink, he worked the straps of her suit off her shoulders. "I want to do it for you."

She stood compliantly while he peeled the suit down. Normally she'd have closed her eyes, transported herself to a realm where she was supremely confident, but she liked seeing the pleasure in Tucker's expression as he revealed her body. His delight was genuine. He made her believe she was the beautiful woman that others had told her she was. One look from him meant as much as all the encouraging words.

She placed her hands to span his hipbones. "I want to do it for you, too."

His arousal had visibly grown, but even without that evidence she'd have known how excited he was by the flinch of his skin and the heated energy that rolled off him. Most of the mud had washed away, but his shorts were still weighted down and she had to push at the sodden material to slide it past his buttocks. She stepped closer, panting with effort in the humidity, until the trunks suddenly dropped away, landing on the floor of the shower stall with a wet slap.

The intimacy heightened. She stayed where she was and palmed his rounded glutes, entranced by the way his erection twitched against her lower belly. He was slick and firm and so very warm. There was such a deep, intrinsic satisfaction in exploring his male body, making him groan, feeling him throb, that she couldn't imagine ever getting enough of it.

This was what she'd been missing in her life. Independence was all well and good, but she would always be wanting more of this moment with Tucker.

Pelted by the spray, they shared a long, luxurious kiss. He slid his hand down the back of her swimsuit, which was hanging around her hips. He stroked the seam of her backside, then reached farther to slide two fingers through the wet folds and stroke her from the inside, as well.

Dizzy with escalating desire, she clung to his waist. Her knees were giving out. "I have to—I have to—" Collapse.

Suddenly his fingers withdrew and he straightened. "Dammit. We don't have condoms."

"What?"

"I didn't think ahead."

"But—"

"We have to get back to our room."

"In this state?" She was incredulous. "I can barely stay on my feet. And what about you?" She took a swaying step back and looked at his rearing erection. The helmeted head was red and ripe, ready to burst.

Daring flowed through her veins, propelling her to take him in her hand. "My turn."

He sucked air through his teeth. "We're not having turns, remember?"

"I misspoke." She gripped the shaft with a new-found assurance and gave him the kind of squeezing stroke that would make it impossible for him to think of anything but finding relief. "This will be my *pleasure.*"

Slowly she lowered to one knee, being sure to drag her hard nipples along his skin. The resulting sensation gave her an idea and she lifted her breasts, capturing his penis between them.

The burning light in Tucker's eyes flared high. "Rory…"

"You like this," she said throatily, taunting him a little as she swayed forward and back, caressing his hot, wet flesh with her own.

He braced one hand against the stone wall and hunched, bending his knees to get the best angle. He held himself still for a moment. The muscles in his flanks trembled, the tendon and sinew strung taut. And then he let out a guttural moan of surrender and pumped his hips, sliding between her breasts in several short jabs.

Rory felt wild. Wanton. She might do *anything*.

She sank onto both knees and took his erection in her hands. It pulsed with vitality and she knew that she wanted to feel the thrust of him in her mouth. Wanted to take him to the ultimate conclusion.

The beating water had removed all traces of mud, but she worked her fingers along the length of him, anyway, lifting and lightly squeezing his sac. Tucker's fingers plunged into her hair and she rested her head against his thigh for a moment, letting him cradle her before she moved in for the kill.

She pointed her tongue like an arrow and licked a straight line up along the underside until she'd reached the head. After making a broad swipe around the rim, she opened her mouth wide and took him in, deeply, swallowing convulsively. He muttered something unintelligible. Rocking on his heels, he pressed both hands to the sides of her skull, holding her firmly but gently, giving her both encouragement and caution.

She inhaled through her nose and offered a grunt of inducement as she wiggled forward on the slick tiles. Slowly he pushed deeper, and she took him, widening her jaw until she'd reached her limit.

She took a quick glance at Tucker through her lashes, but his eyes were closed, his features knotted with intense absorption. Driven to suck hard, she rose up slightly and reached back and gripped his flexing buttocks. The raw eroticism was not a frequent experience for her. She wanted it all—the scent and taste of aroused male, the water sheeting silver over his stomach, the rhythm and thrust and passion and even her humble position.

Suddenly, Tucker withdrew. "Rory, we can't."

She grasped his thighs, her nails digging in so he wouldn't tear himself away. "Why?"

His words were ragged. "It's not—I want to…to keep you safe—"

Water pelted her upturned face, running into her mouth. "I understand, but…" She smacked her lips, swiped at the droplets dripping off her chin, contemplating the unrelieved extent of his arousal. The man had the willpower of a saint. Did he care for her that much?

"Get up here." He hoisted her off the floor. "Before I lose control."

"I'm safe," she said. "I'm healthy."

"So am I, but even so…"

"There are other options." She pushed her suit off and kicked it away, moving in to worm her body against his, rising and squirming until his erection was trapped between her thighs. One thrust and he'd be inside her.

He struggled to maintain control, holding on to her shoulders. "Listen. Our first time should be in a proper bed, right? Soft music, low lighting." With a moan, he gave in to her embrace and wrapped his arms around her. "Pillows to cushion your sweet body."

"Oh, Tucker. I'm touched. Are you a secret romantic?"

"I want everything to be right for you."

"This *is* right."

"Except the lack of condoms."

"You could pull out."

He hesitated. "That's not one-hundred-percent safe, even if I could manage to do it once I'm…there."

She took his hand and slipped it between their bellies. "Right *here*. Feel me."

He stroked at her cleft, not teasing this time, but pinpointing her center of pleasure, sending licks of fire shooting outward from the tight bead of nerve endings. "I need this," she begged, standing on tiptoe with trembling legs, trying to slide herself onto his rock-hard shaft. "You need it. Please, please, just put your cock inside me."

Another deep groan was wrenched from his chest. "You're not thinking this through."

"No, and it's wonderful."

"It's dangerous." He pressed her against the wall of the shower room, his fingers going where his erection wouldn't. "I won't do it."

She went up on her toes, dying to feel him take her with one fierce and fluid stroke. But the refusal in his face was even stronger than her mindless need. Later, she'd be grateful. Now, she was only frustrated.

Tucker shuddered against her. "This feels good, but it'll be even better later."

"I know." Her hips rocked, her insides squeezing down on his fingers as the pressure and pleasure inside her expanded. "I know…I know…"

"I can't hold off much longer."

She clasped at him. "Just a little while."

He took possession of her mouth with a hungry kiss, working his hips to grind against her, the heel of his hand putting an exquisite tugging tension on her clit as he cocked a leg to part her slippery thighs. Their tongues mated. The huge hunger inside her cracked apart, becoming a savage careening ecstasy that crashed through her like an earthquake.

For one instant he froze, his hands cradling her ass. Then he relaxed his grip and she slithered onto her feet again. "No," she whispered, although she knew he'd done the right thing by refusing to make love to her without protection. The loss seemed immense, even so.

She held his head in a tender embrace as he pressed his face against her shoulder, bunched his shoulders and jerked in several short, hard spasms, releasing the jetting warmth of his climax. They stayed like that for several minutes, washed by the streaming water, needing each other for support as the adrenaline and primitive instinct drained from their bodies.

At last they disengaged, though not entirely. Rory wanted to keep a hand on him, or feel the brush of his leg or arm or mouth; she wasn't ready to break contact and, even worse, couldn't imagine a time when she would be.

He dunked under the shower spray, then emerged, giving his head a shake. His expression was bleak. "That was the hardest thing I ever did, saying no."

"Thank you for having the willpower. I didn't."

"It was still dangerous, even though I didn't come inside you."

Dangerous in several ways, she acknowledged. The practical consideration was one thing, but at the moment what she worried most about was the risk to her heart. She was at least halfway in love with him already, and now this? Another night together and she'd be over the moon.

"I'm sure it'll be okay," she said. "We didn't get *that* close. The chances of there being a problem are one in a zillion."

He looked at her with indecipherable eyes. "All the same, you'll let me know?"

"Of course. There's absolutely nothing to worry about, thanks to you keeping your cool." When she'd begged him not to.

"Didn't feel that way to me." He grinned, wiping a hand over his wet face. "Be sure to hold on to my number, anyway."

"Yeah, sure." *That was all he had to say? The weekend wasn't even over and he was already setting up their separation.*

She was baffled, then annoyed at herself for caring so much. This wasn't, after all, a love affair.

Still, she wondered. *This is all I get?*

Tucker took a deep breath. "I want you to know that I...I—"

I love you, she said to him with every inch of her body except her voice.

"I'd do the right thing," he finished. "In case of that one-in-a-zillion chance." He traced a fingertip beneath her bottom lip, his eyes softer now. "That's a promise. You can count on me."

Because he was a good and honorable man beneath the happy-go-lucky veneer, she thought. Not because he couldn't live without her.

Good thing there was nothing to be concerned about as far as pregnancy went, because she suddenly understood that she wasn't settling for less than true love.

11

"I NEED TO GET things straight in my mind," Rory murmured to herself, apparently thinking she was alone.

Tucker stood in the doorway to the bedroom, watching her. After their near miss in the mud baths, they'd returned to the room to change for dinner, avoiding discussion of the growing feelings between them. He'd probably come off badly with his blunt insistence that she call him on the minuscule chance that they'd made too much contact. But he hadn't wanted there to be anything left to chance...or interpretation. His father and older brothers had pounded the need for safety into him. If that failed, full responsibility.

And he still remembered Rory's expression when she'd talked of babies. He even wondered, after his mind had cleared, if her willingness to proceed without a condom had been a subconscious attempt at wish fulfillment.

Maybe that's what she was debating right now.

"I wouldn't mind straightening us out, either," he said, coming into the room with the bottled water she'd requested. He flopped down on his stomach beside her on the bed. "But what's crooked?"

She blinked. "Not you, I hope."

"You have to question that?"

"This playboy reputation—" She waved her hands. "What's that about?"

"What makes you think I'm a player? Have I tried to manipulate or trick you into sleeping with me?"

"No." She stroked a hand over his shoulder. "The opposite, in fact. I've been pleasantly surprised by your manners and thoughtfulness—except when you're teasing me."

"I was raised right. My brothers and sisters are to blame for the teasing tendency. As a group, we don't take life too seriously until there's a real need to. Then we always come through for each other. Always."

"I like that." He reached up and took her hand. She smiled though her eyes remained serous. "Are we being serious now?" she asked softly.

"If you want."

"All I want is to know that you won't hurt me. I'm not asking for promises. That's not the point of this weekend." Burrowed within a puffy comforter and king-size pillows, she wormed closer to him, pulling their clasped hands under her chin as she touched her head to his. The fingers of her other hand played in his hair, sending prickles over his scalp.

"It's always been my intention not to hurt you," he said. "That's why I've hesitated for so long."

"Do you have any worries that maybe *I'll* hurt *you*?"

He hadn't looked at it that way. Why?

"I'm not so vulnerable," he said.

"Tough guy?"

"Not really. But I don't open up easily."

Her breath was warm on his ear. "Why's that?"

"Would you believe if I said I'd had a hard-knock life? No? Then maybe it's just because I'm a man."

She dropped her face against his shoulder and sighed. "I thought you were about to finally admit to a broken heart that never mended."

"Sorry. There are no deep psychological traumas in my life. I've struggled to find my place like everyone, and maybe I'm not completely satisfied with all my choices, but I have few complaints. You were right, you know. I've never been in love."

"That's too bad. In fact, that might even be a complaint."

"Yeah?"

"Yeah."

"Not a complaint," he said. "Though it might be something to look forward to, with the right girl."

Rory placed a small kiss on his cheek. "I hope you find her."

"Maybe I already have," he said, stunned by his own admission and reverting to playfulness before she could reply. He took her by the arms and rolled her over onto her back, climbing atop her and instantly moving his hands up to her head to hold her in place while he thoroughly kissed her. "This is a new variation of the Schulz brothers' headlock," he said between kisses, adding, "Dreaded in six states," as he settled himself more heavily when she laughed and bucked against his weight. "Combined with a very gentle body slam."

"Ah, but you don't need to subdue me," she purred,

working her arms free and wrapping them around his upper body. "I've been waiting all weekend to get in this position with you."

"Finally we're here."

He looked down. The tops of her breasts swelled above the V neckline of her dress. Her scent intoxicated him, a combination of perfume and warm womanly flesh. He inhaled deeply before dropping a kiss at the top of her cleavage, his tongue snaking out to lick along the plump seam.

She made a sound of pure enjoyment. He returned to her mouth, wanting to capture the pleasure and hold it between them to savor. They were in no rush this time. He could take all night long to love her as carefully and exhaustively as she deserved. No more joking, no more questions. Only their naked bodies and all the bliss they could consume.

Their clothes came off in leisurely fashion, both of them more concerned with kissing and caressing the body parts they revealed than moving on without a thorough exploration. She was ticklish behind her knees. He was more sensitive at the small of his back than he'd ever imagined, especially when she scraped him with her teeth, then followed with a lick of her pointed tongue and a quick plucking kiss.

Eventually they had worked their way back to the original position. He had a hand on each of her breasts and was slowly rolling her nipples, matching the movement with the circling of his hips. Her legs were open to him and he felt how warm and wet she was right through the latex of the condom he wore. Each gliding motion of her welcoming thrusts made him, impossibly, even larger and harder.

Rory's head was flung back, her expression enraptured. "Now, Tuck. Please say I don't have to wait anymore because that's just not possible."

He didn't answer in words. One fluid motion was enough as her body opened to him, all the way, tightly clasping his cock in the promised heat. The satisfaction as he bottomed out was visceral and complete, exactly what he'd wanted—craved—from almost the very beginning.

"*This* is how I imagined it," he said, smoothing strands of damp hair off her forehead. Lodged deep inside her, looking directly into her eyes, he literally felt a new connection was being forged between them. Was this what intimacy was about? He was no longer sure why he'd avoided it, until he remembered Sam saying something about how he'd understand when the right woman came along.

It was true. Being with Rory was different. He wanted to live up to her expectations, even though up to now she'd been scrupulous about keeping this weekend casual as promised.

That promise seemed a long time ago.

"Just me and you," he said, rocking their bodies in the mounded pillows. "In a big soft bed. Taking our time, nice and slow."

Her face was peaceful now, her eyes half closed. A small smile lifted the corners of her lips as she stroked one palm along his shoulder blade. "Nice and sweet and slow."

"Yeah." He let out a long breath, squeezed her lush body, telling himself not to get carried away and forget the plan to maintain the status quo. Rory was compliant. He had no reason to change direction now and start thinking about what it would be like to fall in love.

No reason? The reason was lying beneath him—round, soft, strong, proud. Honey eyes, lips like plump grapes, a body that wouldn't quit, a mind that fascinated him and a laugh that lit up his world.

He should tell her.

But she was so calm. She breathed evenly and deeply, only the tiny flutter of her eyelids betraying what was happening down low where her thighs fell open and he pushed minutely deeper inside her liquid warmth.

Unsure about what he was feeling, but not what to do, he dropped his mouth to her breast and took hold of one of her nipples, smiling when he thought of her out by the pool, asking him, with a wide-eyed amazement, to please her.

She arched toward his mouth. "Ohhh, Tucker. You know I love that."

"I could do this forever," he whispered against her breast. Her skin was faintly marbled like an old ivory statue, but warm and soft and giving.

She smiled dreamily. "Surely that's not too much for me to ask for."

"The hotel bill would be wicked."

"I'd pay any price."

He cupped her breast, making it plumper for his

mouth. There was so much to her, but he would never get enough.

They stayed like that for what seemed like a long time, languid and easy, kissing and caressing, joined as one. Eventually the urge to pump grew too strong to hold back. She rolled her hips beneath him. His breathing became labored as he waited, waited, trying to drag out each moment of pleasure.

"Mmm." She bit down on her bottom lip. "Yes. That's so—mmm."

"Deeper?" he asked, crooking a leg to push himself solidly against her.

She tightened around him. "A little deeper. Harder."

Their pace increased.

Her legs pulled up. A ripple went through her.

He pressed a finger to her clit, rubbing in a circle, and she let out a little scream before pulling a pillow over her face.

"Love it," she mumbled into the crushed pillow.

His head came up. "What?"

"What you're doing. I love it. Keep touching me. I'm almost—oh—" She gasped. "Almost there."

He continued stroking. By hand, by cock. Stroking her over the edge, holding on to her at the same time, capturing her flailing hands as she flung the pillow and arched to meet the same soaring sensation that had lifted him into the stratosphere. Fingers knitted, he pushed her hands down on either side of her fanned hair and drove into her. Fast strokes shortening to the final push.

One, two, three and then came the delirious rush.

The tension leached out of him and he slowed, gradually stopping, but not extricating himself. She hugged him to her, burbling like a dove. Nonsense words, but he knew the meaning.

Tell her.

Tell her you want her.

But he wasn't ready. He had to prove himself to her first, make her see that he was a better man than she'd assumed, that he had prospects and wasn't only a careless bachelor with no ambition.

Pulling that off would be some trick.

He planted kisses across her forehead, working his way to her pinkened cheeks, her closed lids. "So was that good for you?" he murmured near her ear.

Her exhale fanned his shoulder. "Uh-huh. I don't know which I like better—fast or slow."

"Slow. Lasts longer."

A lazy laugh tumbled out of her. "But fast means we can do it twice in the same amount of time."

"Why debate? Both are good."

She twisted her head and rocked her shoulders, limbering herself. "I can't believe we wasted so much time trying to decide what this weekend should entail."

He fingered the healthy curve of her butt. "En*tail*?"

"Oh, stop it. I'm trying to be objective and adult here."

"Then I guess now's not the time to compliment your fandamntastic hooters."

She punched his upper arm. "You big goon. Don't try to distract me with that nonsense. I've got your number."

His kissed her chin before rolling away. "We don't need to analyze this."

"I suppose not. What's happened is quite clear."

"Oh?" He wondered if she felt the way he did, or if the deep desire he'd sensed in her was simple neediness, directed at him because he was conveniently *here*.

"Great sex," she said, looking obliquely at him from beneath her lashes.

"Of course."

Tomorrow, he'd tell her. When they got back to the city, he would look at her without the fantasy fogging his vision and then he'd know if they, as a couple, were real.

He'd figure out if he had a genuine chance with her.

NINETY MINUTES into the drive home, Tucker was glowering and Rory was regretting that she'd turned her cell phone on to get her messages. It had been off all weekend. She'd left instructions at Lavender Field that she could be contacted through the resort only in a case of dire emergency.

Tucker had no business being miffed. She'd turned to the phone because she'd assumed they were done. He'd been preoccupied on the drive, monosyllabic toward her attempts at conversation, focused only on the road. So she'd taken out the phone to receive her voice mail. Several messages in—Lauren, Mikki and her mother all giving various versions of "You go, girl!"— she'd learned that Katya, the Chestnut Street store manager, had considered a fire at the new store a *minor* emergency.

Six calls later, Rory was reassured. She'd talked to

Katya, the contractor, the electrician, the fire inspector, then Katya and the contractor again. Finally she put the phone away.

Tucker gave a questioning grunt. "Fire?"

Me, Caveman.

Rory was determined to remain friendly, even if he felt the need to withdraw. "There was a small electrical fire at the new store. Everything's under control."

"Electrical?"

"They suspect that there was a problem with some unfinished wiring. Luckily it happened while workers were there, so they put it out quickly. There was smoke damage to the new drywall. I freaked a bit at that— well, you heard. But, Roger, my contractor, assured me that repairs will only take a day or so. The date for the grand opening is safe."

"If you pass inspection," Tucker muttered.

"What?"

"Sounds like your electrician is incompetent."

"He's not, I assure you," she said, striving for conviction. "You think?"

Tucker shrugged.

She started to reach for her bag to get the phone out again, then forced herself not to. The fire had been minor, they'd all reassured her. No sense in reverting to panic mode just because Tucker felt like being gloomy.

The fog that had clouded the view for the first part of their drive had dissipated, leaving a sky of flannel clouds edged in blue. She leaned her arm on the open window and rested her chin on it, watching the white specks of herons in the surf.

"Should we stop for dinner?" she said into the wind.

Tucker didn't hear her.

She cut her eyes away from him and back to the view. The wind rushed by. "Should we stop for sex?" she added. Out loud, to amuse herself.

After a minute Tucker answered. "I thought we'd push straight through."

She bolted upright. He'd heard her?

Both questions?

"Uh, you're not hungry?" she asked, trying to keep her gaze aimed forward.

He was smiling to himself, but she caught that out of the corner of her eye, relieved he'd come out of the funky mood. "My appetite's been sated."

She inhaled, then turned slinkily—that was, as slinkily as she could manage when strapped in by a seat belt. "Which appetite do you mean?"

"Wasn't the question about food?"

She stopped slinking. Maybe he *hadn't* heard her.

His gaze flickered, jumping away from the road. "Or did you want to eat something else?"

"What did you have in mind?" She snapped out of the belt and slid over next to him, putting her hand on his thigh.

His muscle flexed beneath her fingers. "You answer first."

She whispered into his ear, telling him exactly what she wanted to do with her mouth and giving a tug on his lobe for emphasis.

His eyes glazed over. The car shimmied and he steadied the wheel, giving his head a quick shake. He swallowed. "Go on."

She was massaging his thigh. "Can you keep your eyes on the road?"

"I'm trying."

"Then…" She reached for the growing bulge beneath his fly. "I would start by sliding my tongue all over your body because I love the taste of you. I'd play with your nipples—get them to stick out like hard little pebbles. I'd turn you on so hard your muscles would feel like stone slabs and every drop of blood in you would rush straight to your dick. You'd get hard as steel." She kneaded him through his jeans. Her fingers were deft and strong; an erection sprang up beneath them. Hmm, turned out that pummeling bread dough was more than therapy—it was a valuable skill.

Tucker had slowed the car, but he was managing to keep them on a steady course.

Not for much longer, she decided, certain that he would pull over before her wicked intentions entered the danger zone. "Remember the mud bath? The shower?" One flick of her thumb and his jeans came unsnapped. "How I was down on my knees, taking you into my mouth? My throat?"

He murmured consent, getting the glazed expression again. Men were so easily distracted.

Chuckling, she tugged at the tab of his zipper. "What a shame we didn't get to finish that."

He groaned, tensely negotiating a wide turn. "Rory, do you want me to drive us off the cliff?"

"Of course not. But maybe this is a test. All you have to do is keep your head while I give it to you."

She ducked under his arm, careful to avoid the gearshift.

A car horn blared at them from a passing vehicle and Tucker sped up again on a straight stretch. The wheels hummed, the car vibrated beneath them. Daring pulsed through her, urging her to reach inside his open fly and ease out his erection.

"Oh, hell," he said. "You can't do this."

"Yes, I can." She rubbed her thumb over the seeping tip. His hips canted and his thighs spread, giving her better access. "Sorry," she said as her elbow dug into his thigh. She had one knee up beneath her and his arm lay against her back, reaching for the wheel. Her head bumped against it and he made a quick correction. Fear skipped inside her.

This is insane, she thought.

So not her.

Which was a damn good reason for continuing.

"Seriously," he warned. But he did nothing to stop her.

So she opened her mouth and took him in, her cheeks hollowing with the suction as she pulled on his swelling flesh.

His leg jumped beneath her as he slammed on the brakes. They pulled over with a screech of tires. A shower of pebbles peppered the undercarriage. She was knocked around by the sudden stop, but she continued going down on him with her lips thinned over her teeth to keep him from injury.

"Damn, Rory." Tucker shoved the gearshift into park and cut the engine.

On an upstroke, she risked a glance over the dashboard. They were parked nose-first at the guardrail of a scenic bypass. "Parking brake," she said thickly before dropping down again.

He leaned forward and set the lever, then collapsed into the seat, slumping lower on his spine. "You're hell on wheels." His right hand wandered over her back, finding the loose hem where her shirt had pulled out of her skirt. "I don't know if I should stop you or make you finish."

Make her? A glugging sound of protest got trapped in her throat.

A car zipped by. He craned his neck after it, then relaxed again. "We could be arrested for public indecency."

She bobbed up, popping off him with a *smack*. "Pretend you're enjoying the view."

"I am," he said with an obvious leer as he flipped up the back of her skirt.

She tried to shimmy it down again, but he wasn't having that. His hand slipped beneath the elastic of her panties and rubbed her backside as if it needed burnishing. The caresses made her squirm and lift her butt higher. He could buff her like a trophy and she'd love it.

"Don't distract me," she muttered. "We have to be quick."

He'd cupped her mound, one knuckle curled to burrow deeper. "Bet I can make you come first."

She paused, staring openmouthed, riveted by his touch. "Stakes?" she rasped.

His eyes darkened. "The necklace."

"Why would you want—"

"So I can have a new key made."

Her heart leaped.

He smiled wickedly. "Winner takes all."

SHE SAT ON THE HOOD, he leaned nearby, both of them staring at the ocean from the scenic overlook he'd pulled into so abruptly that the tires had left gouges in the dirt.

They were roughly seventy-five miles outside of San Francisco. Scarlet poppies waved in the breeze. Gulls cawed overhead. The moment appeared deceptively tranquil. Actually, Tucker was waiting for the blood to return to his brain. Rory seemed to be breathing in time to the rhythmic swell and dip of the waves, though heavier than normal.

She worried at her necklace, pulling it back and forth between the point of her collar. "I've been thinking, and there's something I should have said earlier."

Sonovabitch. Here it came. She'd decided he was a fun screw, but not on her level socially.

"I've got to explain," she said, stalling.

"Don't bother." He swung his toe at the tire of her expensive convertible. "I get it."

Her brows went up. "What do you get?"

"That the weekend's almost over and so are we."

"I wasn't going to say that." Her voice became soprano. "Not at all!"

Because she was a kind person, sensitive to injured pride. Not like Charla, or the type of woman he'd run into so often in the past that he'd stopped going to the trendy bars—the women who thought he was good for a one-night stand, but not up to snuff when they quizzed him about what kind of car he drove and how much money he made. Their faces always fell when he said he was an electrician.

Rory's hadn't, he remembered. But then, she'd been raised to accept all sorts of people.

Turned out he wanted more than acceptance from her. And she'd already questioned his lifestyle a few times. The instances had been minor and he'd thought he'd brushed them off, but they'd stuck under his skin like a burr under a saddle.

She'd frowned at his flexible schedule and laid back attitude toward work.

She'd insisted on taking her car this weekend, then offered to pay extra expenses.

She'd ordered the wine at dinner when he took too long trying to decipher the list.

Small instances, but big implications.

"Now that you brought it up…" Rory's voice wobbled and he damned his quick assumption. "I suppose we do have to talk about what happens when we get back to the city."

"What do you want to happen?" he asked carefully.

She cleared her throat, dropping her timbre into normal range. "I was thinking we'd be friends."

"But not lovers."

"I don't know." Her eyes narrowed as she looked at him, the wind throwing her hair into a flyaway tangle. She raised a hand to pull a piece of it out of her mouth.

"You're the one who said from the start that we couldn't do both."

"I don't remember it that way."

"You claimed it'd be awkward, seeing each other around. Especially now that we know Mikki and Nolan will probably stay together and there's no way we can avoid each other."

"I said that before we became friends first."

She furrowed. "I'm getting confused. What is it you expect from me, back home?"

"Does this have to be an either/or choice?"

There was a long silence, but the light in Rory's eyes—a dazzle of gold—gave him hope. Or maybe that was only a reflection of the sun and he was fooling himself.

She leaned a shoulder into him. "Can we possibly be friends *and* lovers?"

"Maybe. If you don't mind that I'm who I am."

"Mind? I love who you are."

His gut clenched at her vehemence, but he couldn't quite believe it'd be so easy. "That's not exactly what I meant."

She made a face. "I know, I know. Too early to be using any permutation of the L-word."

"Unless you're referring to lust," he said, needing to lighten the mood. He had some thinking to do, some plans to make, some work to accomplish.

Her grin was wry. "One thing we know for sure after this weekend is that we can always fall back on lust."

"And fall into it."

"On top of it."

"Swallow it whole." He winked.

Blushing, she reached for the necklace and worked the chain around her neck until the clasp was at the front. She looked down, frowning as she fiddled with it.

"I'll do it," he offered, but the necklace came free.

She held it high, watching the suitcase charm spin in a small circle. "I hate to give this up, but you won it fair and square."

"You'll have to practice your technique," he teased.

Her lips pursed at the implied challenge. "Rematch?"

"Any time you say the word."

He held out his palm.

She dropped the necklace into it. "Take care of it."

He opened his mouth to say, *As if it were your heart,* but he couldn't. He wasn't that kind of guy.

Yet.

_12_

RORY HAD BEGUN to wonder if her time with Tucker at Painter's Cove six days ago had been only a dream. A fantasy.

The X-rated kind.

Never to be repeated.

"You're staring at that butter funny," Lauren observed. She and Mikki had descended for their usual Saturday morning gab-'n-nosh-fest in the kitchen of Lavender Field. "Has it gone off?"

Rory blinked. "Nope, our butter is always farm-fresh." She shut the door of the Sub-Zero fridge and returned to the stools they'd pulled up to the work counter, holding out the covered dish. "But I don't want any. Here, take it."

"You must be on the Lovesick Diet," Mikki said, rescuing the butter. "I always lose and gain the same five pounds, according to the status of my love life."

Lauren nodded in approval. "I thought you'd been at the gym. Your thighs are so toned."

"I've been working out, all right." Mikki slapped her bare leg beneath a pair of threadbare denim cutoffs. The reinstated wedding ring glinted on her left hand. "Riding Nolan."

Lauren twirled an imaginary lasso overhead. "Yippee ki-yi-aye."

"Is a second honeymoon in order?" Rory asked, smiling behind the faience mug holding her first coffee of the day even though she'd been up since dawn, baking bread and running through the grand opening to-do list in her head. She hadn't even thought of food.

Mikki preened, tucking her shining black hair behind her ears and adjusting the plunging neckline of her halter top. The special sparkle in her eyes had become a permanent fixture. "We're thinking about it."

"Try Painter's Cove." Lauren broke open one of her favorite blueberry-cheese croissants. "The place did wonders for Rory."

"The four of you could double book and have yourselves a regular old key-partner sex marathon," Rory joked, not wanting to get into the discussion about her and Tucker. Not only had Lauren recently scored her dream job with *Left Coast* magazine, but she'd smoothed over the bumps in her relationship with Josh McCrae. They were planning to move in together.

At the news, Maureen Baxter had acquired quite the ego about the success ratio of her key party. She couldn't understand why Rory was holding out.

Neither could Rory.

Mikki zeroed in on her sister's reticence. "What about you and Tuck? Has he called?"

"We've talked a couple of times."

"And?" Lauren prodded.

"And I think we're back to being friends."

"Oh, no." Mikki was obviously distressed; she'd

been planning on mutual dinner parties, couples' bar-becues and family beach outings. "What makes you say that?"

Rory shrugged. "There's no heat left, now that we did the deed."

"You can't be sure over the phone."

"Yes, you can. He hasn't asked me out. That's a damn good indicator." She skipped over how Tucker had hung out at Lavender Field for an hour on Friday, shooting the breeze like a buddy, until she'd had to leave for her drawing class. He'd walked her to her car and said a casual goodbye, without asking her if she was posing. There was no mention of seeing her again, either. No mention of fitting together their lock and key.

"Why don't *you* ask him?" With polished nails, Lauren picked a pastry flake off her vintage forties polka-dot blouse. "Don't revert to the shy Rory."

Shy? Rory nearly choked. "It's way too late for that."

Lauren smiled. "Tucker's probably waiting for you to make the next move."

Rory remembered how he'd eschewed the common practice of you-do-me-and-I'll-do-you. "Tucker's not like that. He doesn't count turns. He doesn't play games—"

Mikki sputtered around a bite of a cinnamon crois-sant.

Rory turned to her. "Is there something you know that I don't?"

"I thought that we'd already established that Tucker's, um, y'know—a player."

"Not with me." Rory was resolute, especially because in her mind players were always slick and smarmy and practiced. Tucker was not.

But suddenly she wondered. What if he'd lost interest and the casual conversations of the past six days were all about letting her down easy? Lord knew, she didn't have the greatest track record for reading men's goodbye signals.

"Anyway, I've been busy," she said briskly, rising to remove several loaves of bread from the oven, banana oatmeal and herbed cornbread. The aroma of baking bread was usually a tonic better than meditation or chocolate, but for once she had no appreciation for it. She dumped the loaves on the cooling racks she'd placed on the butcher block, all business.

"She's making bread," Mikki said out of the side of her mouth to Lauren.

"Not a good sign."

"I'm nervous about the grand opening next Friday," Rory said. "We're running a sale at all of the stores Friday through Sunday, so it's been an extra hassle seeing that we're fully stocked. The bakery manager had to hire extra workers. Then there's the new store. The electrical fire, I mean, flare-up, put us behind schedule. I've been scrambling to rearrange my schedule so I have time to go in and set up the decor at the last minute."

"That's a long explanation." Lauren popped a curved slice of honeydew melon into her mouth.

"It's a long list of chores." Rory blamed the fluttery feeling in the pit of her stomach on the assault against her need for order. "I'm counting on you two helping out with the last-minute details. Nothing too strenuous, since I've booked a decorative painter to do the walls and beams." As in all of her stores, the walls would be plastered like an old French farmhouse and the beams similarly aged and stained. "Y'know, hanging a few bundles of lavender, unpacking the pottery, that kind of thing."

"Of course we'll help," Mikki said. "I still owe you for coming through with all those pastries for the key party."

"What about Mom?" Lauren suggested.

"I'm avoiding Mom."

"How come?"

"You know how she is. She'll take charge." The truth was, Rory feared that Emma would take one look in her eyes and know she'd fallen in love. She might be able to deflect her sisters' scrutiny, but she could never fool her mother.

"That's true enough," Lauren said with a nod. "But at least you'd know that everything would be finished on time with her in charge."

"There must be new tables and chairs to arrange. I'll ask Nolan to come and give us a hand with the heavy lifting." Mikki smiled slyly. "And I'll bet Tucker would love to help, too. Has he volunteered?"

One of the workers, clad in the store's signature lavender apron, came into the kitchen to use the bread-slicing machine. "We're running low on sourdough," she said cheerfully, "and Julio's new focaccia has completely sold out."

"Shoot," Mikki said, "I wanted to bring one home.

Nolan's making some kind of healthy vegetable stir fry tonight and I'll need bread with it or else I'll be mowing through the pantry at midnight."

Rory went to the phone. "I can have a focaccia sent over from the main bakery, or delivered to your house, if you'd rather. Lauren, how about you? I'll bet Viv is missing the steady supply of sourdough rolls now that you've moved out." Viv and Lauren had been sharing an apartment since college. But now they both had new roommates—of the romantic variety.

Before either sister could answer, the phone rang, almost under Rory's hand. She lifted the receiver. "Lavender Field. How may I help—"

"Rory, it's Roger." Her contractor. "Don't panic, but we're having a serious problem."

"Not another fire, I hope," she said. Her sisters leaned forward to listen in.

"Nothing like that. But it's bad enough. The city inspector was here yesterday for the final inspection and he wouldn't green-light the new breaker box the electricians put in after the fire. Incomplete work, he says. I've got a generator coming back in for temporary power, so we should be able to finish most of our work this weekend as promised, but, uh…"

"Go ahead, spit it out."

"I can't get hold of the electrician. No one at Scully and Sons is picking up. I've left a dozen messages."

"Shit. How bad is this?"

"Well, you need the occupancy permit to open up, of course, to say nothing of the lack of power."

"If we can get the electricians back, how long will the fix take?"

"Can't say for sure, but it should be doable, providing—"

"Providing they're competent. At this point, that's a long shot I'm not willing to take." Rory gnawed at her lip.

"Sorry. This company was a new subcontractor for me. I won't be hiring them again."

"Roger, I know someone we can get. He's reliable."

"Great. Give me his number."

"Um, let me handle that. You just hold down the fort at the store. Do what you can for now to keep progress moving forward. I am *not* postponing my opening date. The newspaper ads are already set."

"We'll make it. If your guy doesn't work out, I've got others to try. Trouble is, they'll charge emergency prices."

"Money is no object. I want the job done right." She got off the phone and rapidly filled her sisters in on the latest crisis. "What do you think? Should I call Tucker?"

"Absolutely," said Mikki.

Rory hesitated. "Maybe I should go see him in person instead of calling. Or is that too pushy? I'll be putting him on the spot, either way."

Lauren got up to clear their brunch dishes. "Friends don't mind being imposed on." She rinsed the dishes in the sink, set them aside and flicked her wet fingertips. "Not *too* much."

"Friends," Rory repeated. "Yeah." She'd be appealing to the white-knight aspect of Tuck's personality, and he did have one, despite his propensity to make wisecracks at inopportune moments. Was that smart, considering she was trying to impress him with her detachment? She would *not* be a clingy woman.

"I'll bring him one of the fresh-baked loaves," she decided, pulling out a flat bakery box from the wire storage shelves beneath the counter. "And some of the cinnamon croissants. A piece of the 'Needful Things' cheesecake should seal the deal."

"Taking it out in trade?" Mikki teased.

Rory stopped and considered the flap she was about to fold. "Maybe I shouldn't. I don't want him to feel obligated."

"Why not?" Mikki asked. "Men *like* to do things for their women. It's their protective gene."

"I know how Rory feels," Lauren said. "It's a matter of pride. After Josh printed the article about flash-dating me at the key party, there was no way I'd go to him for a favor."

"But Tuck hasn't done anything wrong," Mikki pointed out.

"He hasn't done anything right, either," Rory muttered. Not since Painter's Cove.

"Go," Mikki said, shooing with her hands. "You've sworn over and over that you would stop second-guessing yourself when it came to men, but I've never seen you follow through. Isn't it time?"

"She's right," Lauren conceded. "You have to believe in Tucker *and* yourself if you want this relationship to work."

"I don't even know his address."

"No prob." Mikki reached for her purse. "I've got it."

Rory snapped open a plastic bag. She'd leave it up to a loaf of banana oatmeal to decide. If Tucker could resist a bread bribe, they had no future, anyway.

"HI, TUCK. It's me…Rory."

"Rory? What's up?"

"Oh, I wondered if you'd mind if I stopped by."

"Here? Now?" She heard him gulp. "I guess that would be okay."

"Is it a bad time?"

"Not if you don't mind messes."

"At my mother's house, I lived with a globby eight-foot-long macramé hanging, a loom the size of a grand piano and at least a half-dozen unfinished craft projects. To say nothing of the dirty dishes a household of kids produce. I can overlook a little mess." She could tell he was reluctant, but she pushed ahead all the same. "I'll be there in sixty seconds."

"Sixty seconds?"

"I'm parked outside your house."

A curtain twitched in a half-moon window of what had to be the basement level of the shabby but genteel row house that matched his address. "So you are," he said. A hand waved. "Hey, there. I'd kill to have your parking luck."

"Where's your truck?"

"Three blocks away."

"We can do the switcheroo when I go." Except she hoped that he'd be leaving with her. Better not count on that, though. The last time she'd counted on a man, she'd wound up with a nine-hundred-dollar lace table-cloth, previously known as her wedding dress.

"C'mon in," Tucker said. "Take the side steps down."

She exited the car, gathered up her offerings—yeast of the gods—and bypassed the front steps that led up to an Edwardian door with faded black paint. A walkway around the corner of the house led to narrow cement steps. At the bottom of the short flight was Tucker, standing in the open door in jeans, work boots and an untucked plaid shirt with the sleeves rolled up past his biceps. One hand held a crowbar and his chest pocket bulged with a tape measure.

"I've interrupted you," she said after they'd exchanged a second greeting.

He pushed at sweat-riddled hair with the back of his hand. "I was just fooling around with a few minor home improvements."

She walked through a dank entrance and into his apartment, trying not to show her shock. *Minor* home improvements? The place looked as though a bomb had gone off.

The plaster on several walls had either fallen or been removed in chunks, revealing the broken strips of lath beneath. Another wall, clearly destined for demolition, still sported water-stained wallpaper with an orange-and-brown geometric pattern circa 1974. The sink of the closet kitchen drained into a bucket.

He had a few acceptable pieces of furniture, primarily a large TV, a brown leather couch and matching armchair. They huddled in the center of the room under a tarp. The dining table was layered with an open pizza box, unidentifiable metal parts—pipes from the sink?—and a week's delivery of the *San Francisco Chronicle.* The remaining decor consisted of a surf-board, a bicycle and a cheaply framed poster of Angelina Jolie as Lara Croft.

The temporary mess she could live with, but bad taste in movies? She shuddered and stepped over a pile of rubble near the door, searching for words. *Nice place* wasn't even remotely possible.

"I was removing part of a wall and an old closet," he said. "To open the place up."

It'd take more than that. Very little light filtered into the rooms. He lived in a rabbit warren. While housing costs in the city were ridiculous, she was dismayed to think that he couldn't afford better.

"I'm sure the improvements will be a…a great improvement."

"I've been busy renovating the other apartments. There are three up above."

"Oh? Do you moonlight as the super?"

"I suppose you might say that, but actually—"

Rory let out a yelp. "Was that a mouse? I saw a mouse! It ran under the pile of broken plaster."

"That's just Joe Montana. He's harmless."

"You name your mice?"

"Only the ones that watch TV with me in the evenings."

"Um, well, I brought you a few baked goods. I hope Joe Montana enjoys them."

Tucker took the Lavender Field boxes. "Thanks. What did I do to deserve this?"

"Good question," she said, taking another wary look around the decrepit apartment.

"I'm really sorry about the mess. I wanted to get the place fixed up before I invited you over."

She blinked. "You did?"

"I don't usually live in squalor, but what happened is that I recently bought this place as an investment with Sam and Didi and we've all been working on it when we can. Me, more than the rest, but my regular clients have kept me busy lately and I haven't made as much progress as I'd hoped."

"You own this, um…"

He gave her the boyishly dimpled smile. "This dump?"

"You're not the super then."

"I'm the landlord, but I guess you could also say I'm the super." He looked at her closely, something dark and cautious in his eyes. "Does that make a difference to you?"

"Yes."

"Huh. At least you're honest."

She lifted her chin. "Am I at fault for preferring a man who's settled?"

He dumped the bakery boxes on the table. "Don't count on me being settled."

"Trust me, I'm not."

The air had grown dense and prickly. She resisted rubbing her hands over her forearms to smooth down the tiny hairs. Rubbing against Tucker, even the wrong way, only made her want to kiss the dickens out of him. His cocky pride aroused her usually well-tamed fighting spirit.

"Can I get you something to drink?" he asked.

"No, thank you."

"I guess there's no reason to bother with a tour. You've seen everything but the bath and bedroom."

"That's okay. I didn't come for a tour."

He approached her, toeing aside a tool box left open in the middle of the room. "Then what did you come for? This?"

His sneak attack was swift and assured. She met him with equal force. Their mouths slammed together in a kiss that was all about feeding their lust for each other. For six days it had been contained, even ignored, but now their need had burst without warning.

"I thought you didn't want me anymore," she panted.

"I always want you." His mouth was hot and sucking; she felt herself drawn into it like a fiery whirlpool.

"Fooled me."

He stopped, pulled back an inch. Glowered at her. "I was being a gentleman."

"Don't be," she said, and grabbed his head with one hand to drag his lips back to hers.

They were wild, voracious. Biting, convulsive, their hands all over each other. Rory's jeans fell to the floor, catching on her sneakers until she kicked them off. Her chambray work shirt held on by one single button while Tucker's hands moved beneath it, shoving her bra up so her breasts swung free.

Being bold and proud of it, she grabbed the plackets

of his shirt and yanked them apart, popping a couple of buttons. She laughed with a reckless joy. *Tucker wanted her! She wanted him. They could be together forever.*

He was stroking her, his hands like rockets, trailing fire. They moved over her, igniting her skin, deepening the heat to a consuming flame as he pulled her against his hips and the hardness there, his tongue licking inside her mouth, licking deeper, hotter, until she was no longer a thinking being but only a creature of sensation and hunger and shocking pleasure.

Tucker kicked open a door. They stumbled into the bedroom and he quickly divested her of her panties. Apparently he'd shed his boots and clothes along the way because when he pushed her down onto the bed and climbed on top of her, he was nude, blatantly engorged, his erection swinging up to slide between her thighs. Suddenly she felt hollow inside. She wanted to take him in—her hands, her mouth, her pussy—and choked on the frustration when he caught hold of her arms and pushed them up over her head, leaving her bra in a tangle around her neck as he tormented her with his wild tongue and burning kisses.

She wound her legs around him, holding him between her open thighs, hoping that the invitation flowing out of her where their hips met would entice him to slide inside her. Her body rocked impatiently against his rigid erection. "I want it," she demanded. "Right away, Tucker."

"You'll get it." He brushed against her and she inhaled at the shock of contact on her aroused sex, but he was only reaching past the bed. Getting a condom.

Thank you, thank you, she chanted inside her head, while the rest of her screamed, *Gimme, gimme.*

Within seconds he was pushing his way into her, as hard and red-hot as a branding iron. She trembled, holding herself still for a moment as he filled her, and then she couldn't stand it and had to move against him, savoring the rugged beauty and strength of his body, the ripple of muscle, the sheen of sweat, the primitive male instinct he exuded like a potent drug, taking all of him into her, too, so that they were truly joined.

A great outpouring of love spilled over her and she didn't know if the emotion had come from her or Tucker or if they'd made it together, sexual alchemists transcending their physical pleasure. The pressure of an impending orgasm built inside her as they moved against each other, but this time the feeling was more than a bodily longing. It was full completion—the ultimate bond.

Tucker was hugging her so hard she had no breath. His face burrowed into her neck as his hips plunged. She pushed back at him, her feet sliding on the sheets as she tried to lift her hips to the pounding pleasure, sinking her fingers in his hair, holding him nearly as tight as he held her.

Her hands clenched.

Her teeth clenched.

Her entire *body* clenched.

"Yes!" she shouted as he rose up on his elbows and drove into her, touching off her climax as he held himself deep inside for a frozen instant of stark and impossible rapture. And then he was exhaling with a moan and lifting her with hands beneath her butt and thrusting again, pulsing with each stroke, over and over, until her climax broke and their muscles gave way and they dropped back to reality in a messy tangle of hot skin and wandering fingers and slippery kisses.

"I didn't think people actually screamed *yes* when they came," she murmured, "but I did. Didn't I?"

"Not sure," he said against her chest. "There was a freight train running through my head."

"I've never, ever, done that before." She stretched, luxuriating in the fullness, the warmth she felt, even in her bones. "Is that pitiful?"

"I'm glad." He dropped kisses over the plump curve where her breast had slipped toward her armpit. "I want it to be the best with me."

"Only you," she promised, before caution could stop her.

Too soon to be talking about exclusivity, her head said, but damn if her body didn't curl toward him, twining him between her legs.

Clinging.

Double damn. Deliberately she unwound herself.

Tucker hadn't seemed to notice her slip. He lifted his head, snagging an arm around her waist when she made a motion to slide away. "Don't leave yet." He turned onto his side and pulled her into the spoon position, his hands splayed over her belly and breast. "Unless you have somewhere to be?"

"Actually…"

His left hand lifted away from her breast.

She clasped it to her. "I came to ask you a favor, Tuck. I didn't expect us to end up in bed."

He'd begun kissing the back of her neck and with a satisfied smile she wondered why she didn't always expect to end up in bed. True, there was the small matter of him giving no indication of the way he felt, but that was a man thing, wasn't it? She assumed he'd been embarrassed about the state of his living quarters, but she'd have to make it clear she'd gone through a few renovations herself and couldn't care less about the upheaval. Although it was touching that he'd wanted to impress her.

"I'll do anything for you," he said.

"Wait until you hear. It's about my new store. The electrician's work didn't pass inspection. I know this is last minute and you probably have other pressing jobs, but if you could at least go there to give me an evaluation of the problem, I would be…I would…"

Her voice died. Not only hadn't he stopped kissing her, but now he was rolling her nipple beneath his thumb, making it hard.

"Sure," he said, breathing against her ear. "I'll clear the time."

"Well." She sighed. "I meant right away. I'd be very grateful."

"Right now is good, too. But does it have to be this very minute?"

His hand had abandoned her breast and insinuated itself between her thighs. She inched them apart and he stroked until his dancing fingertips were at her slick opening.

"Maybe not *right* this minute."

A banging sounded at the door, a mere instant before it was thrown open to thud against the wall. "Hey, Tuck! We're here to help with the demo. Where are ya, man?"

Suddenly, Tucker was no longer the sweet lover. He scrambled out of bed and started flinging the linens around, looking for his clothes. He threw Rory's panties at her. "You have to get out of here. I don't want them to see you."

She flattened her hands over her breasts. "What? Who is it?"

"My brothers."

13

"WHY CAN'T THEY see me?" Rory pulled in on herself, making a defensive face that didn't hide her hurt at the presumed insult. "I mean, of course I don't want them to see me naked, but—"

"It's not like that." Tucker couldn't find his jeans. They had to be in the living room. Rory's, too, he realized.

He crossed to the bureau and pulled out the first garment he grabbed—a pair of zebra-striped jammers. While he yanked them on, he tried to explain. Unfortunately, Sam and Gabe were making a racket in the other room. They'd be poking their noses into the bedroom any second.

"My family—they're nosy. They'll be all over me if they know about you. It'll be easier if we keep this quiet. Okay?"

She shrugged.

Regretfully he watched her boobs get covered by the bra she'd untangled and slipped over her arms. "Why don't you stick around? I'll get rid of these clowns."

She shook her head. "I have to go. But I need my clothes."

"Tuck? You in there?" The door started to open and Tucker shoved it closed. "I'll be out in a sec," he called.

A fist thumped against the door. Sam roared with laughter. "Who you hiding in there?"

Tuck ignored the interruption. "Rory." He kept his voice low. "Don't go."

She looked up at him from the bed, seemingly torn.

He couldn't wait for her answer. The knob was rattling threateningly, although he was fairly certain that they wouldn't actually bust in. Gabe and Sam just liked to act like jerks.

Tuck slipped through and gave them each a push, steering them toward the living room. "You're acting like ten-year-olds. Step back or I'll have to tell your wives."

"They'd be the first to ask us for details," Gabe said, trying to see past Tuck's shoulder even though he'd shut the door.

"Aw, leave the kid alone," Sam said. He circled around the tarp-covered couch, then made a swoop to retrieve an item from the floor. "Well, well, well. Look here."

He held up Rory's jeans and chambray shirt. "Someone stripped before they reached the bedroom."

Tucker moved fast to grab the clothing away. He bunched the garments, holding them tight under one arm. "Hey, look, guys, thanks for stopping by and all, but we'll have to reschedule the demo. My plans for the day have changed. There's somewhere I have to go—"

"Like the bedroom?" Gabe made a feint toward the door.

Tucker pointed, the force of his glare fixing his brother in place as he stalked across the room. "Keep out of there. I am not kidding."

Gabe backed off with his hands in the air. "All right, all right. You don't have to blow your top."

"This one's not a joke."

Gabe and Sam exchanged a sobering look.

Tuck took advantage of their momentary silence to dodge into the bedroom. This time, he locked the door.

The bed was empty.

"Rory?" he called.

She stepped out of the adjoining bathroom, drying her hands on a towel. She'd gone through his drawers and put on one of his T-shirts. It hung at mid-thigh on her bare legs and with an appreciation that felt a lot like a swift kick to the gut he was reminded of how long and gorgeous they were. She had legs with muscle and shape, not sticks that looked as though they'd snap in the wind off the bay.

"Those my jeans?" She came over and liberated them. "I don't suppose you got my shoes."

"No, sorry."

"Are your brothers still here?"

"I think so." No doors had banged shut.

"I'll go out the back way." She nodded at the French doors he'd recently installed to open the dingy flat to the walled courtyard. "So they won't *see me*."

He'd better explain about that later, so she understood that he was protecting her from curious siblings, not the other way around. "What about the job you had for me?"

"You can phone me when you're free."

"But I'm free now."

She gave him a long look. "No, I don't believe you are. At least, not when it comes to me."

"I'M TELLING YOU the truth," Gabe insisted later that day. "I heard him say Rory. That's a guy's name."

"Spare me," Didi said, doing an exasperated eye roll as she looked over the ink drawings laid out on her drafting table. "The name is unisex, like a lot of them these days."

"Then how do you explain the clothes? The jeans and shirt? There was nothing feminine about them. Not even the size."

"You've never seen women in denim before?"

"What I mean is, no frills or sparkles," Gabe said, looking less sure of his conclusions. "They weren't small, either."

"So? Neither are my jeans. *You* could probably fit into them. And frills and sparkles are for tweens, not grown women. Maybe Tuck's new girlfriend has nice child-bearing hips. That'll make Mom happy."

"Yeah, but Tucker's never gone for…uh—"

"If you say 'fatties' I'll stick this pen in your eye."

Gabe had the grace to look sheepish. "You know what I mean. Tuck has always liked little blondes the best."

"Yes, petite blonde *females*."

"I'm just saying it was weird. Whoever it was ran out the back door before we got a peek."

Didi continued to look skeptical. "What did Sam think?"

"He found the shoes."

"So?"

"They were running shoes. Could have been a woman's, I guess. He didn't get a good look at them before Tuck came back and rushed us out the door. There had to be a damn good reason he was so nervous about us seeing who was in his bed."

"And that means it was a man?" Didi could barely stifle her screech of frustration. This was like dealing with the one-track minds of her kids when the only thought in their heads was the cookie jar.

"Well, the evidence—"

"You two are such idiots that I can't imagine how your wives put up with you."

Gabe grunted and leaned back in the chair, folding his arms across his chest. He had to feel fairly strongly about his theory; he'd tracked her down at the office. Or maybe Sam was just fooling with his more gullible sibling and sending him on a fool's errand like the time he'd persuaded both Gabe and Tuck to dye their Little League uniforms puce.

Gabe frowned. "So you don't think it's strange how quiet he's kept his interest in this Rory person?"

Didi *had* wondered about that. Then again, she couldn't blame her baby brother for attempting to secure some privacy. With all the siblings married except Tuck, they had only his sex life to gossip over.

"I'll look into the matter," she said, heaving a sigh as if interfering was a burden. Honestly, her curiosity was roused. There wasn't a snowball's chance in hell that Tuck had become a switch-hitter, but he *was* keeping something from them.

And she had a good idea of what the secret might be.

Her baby brother was in love.

THE GRAND OPENING of the Polk Street store in Russian Hill went off without a hitch. Unless Rory counted the nervous stomach that had her almost bolting in the middle of the ribbon-cutting ceremony. While a city official did the honors, she'd swallowed hard and smiled for a newspaper photographer sent to cover the event. The wide, satin lilac-colored ribbon had given way beneath the scissors and the store was declared open for business. After a polite smattering of applause, the small crowd had rushed the store, enticed by the smell of fresh bread and offers of free samples.

Rory should have gone inside to accept accolades and to oversee the fledgling operation, but she was looking for Tucker. He'd promised to come. Finally she spotted him among those still loitering on the sun-splashed sidewalk. He was talking with Nolan and Mikki.

He'd made it! She was so relieved. At last her butterflies lighted and the squeezing tension eased. She wasn't ready to face what that said about how much she'd come to count on him.

He had been a godsend during the store preparations, meeting with her contractor the Saturday she'd gone to his apartment and then slaving nonstop to fix the shoddy workmanship of the previous electrician. On Monday, the store had passed inspection. By Wednesday, the decorative painter had finished and

Rory had been able to organize a work crew to help her with the finishing details. She'd promised them a movie party as a reward.

Mikki came up and hugged Rory. "Congratulations, sweetie. The store looks great."

Nolan was next, handsome and clean-cut in a button-down shirt and charcoal trousers. "If you ever need investors…"

She kissed his cheek. "I'll be sure to let you know when I go public." He'd taken to teasing her about her transformation from hippie chick to minimogul.

Tucker loomed behind Nolan. He said hello. Rory smiled brightly and was reaching out to give him a hug when he said, "I'd like you to meet my sister."

She stopped with her arms hanging open. Her eyes went to the brown-haired woman at Tuck's elbow. "Oh, wow. Your sister."

"This is Didi Schulz Franklin," he said. "When she heard I was working on the new Lavender Field store, she wangled a ride to the opening."

"I eat more of your cheesecake than any human ought to," Didi said, shaking Rory's hand. She was quite short, and almost squat with a boxy figure clad in wrinkled cotton separates, but there was a relaxed, honest air about her that combined with lively green eyes, a snub nose and an impish smile to give her an aura of attractiveness.

Rory felt an immediate kinship.

Tucker finished the introduction. "Didi, this is Aurora Constable. Everyone calls her Rory. She's the owner of Lavender Field and my very good friend."

"Very good friend," Didi echoed, leaning toward

Rory with an aggrieved air. "As if I don't know what that means."

Rory blinked. "You do?"

"Sure. But I'm under orders from Tuck not to be my usual overbearing self, so I won't be asking what your intentions are or anything like that." Didi grinned. "I hear Sam and Gabe busted in on you two the other day."

"Oh, God." Rory blushed furiously. "Who told you that?"

"One thing you'll soon learn about the Schulzes," said Didi, "we're a gossipy bunch."

Rory shot Tucker a curious look. He returned a bland smile. She might have liked to learn more about—and from—his sister, but they were soon separated in a milling group of new arrivals.

It was another twenty minutes before Rory was able to take a breather. The store was no longer packed, though a line of customers wound around the perimeter of the main room.

"Come with me," Lauren whispered in Rory's ear, taking hold of her arm and towing her to the kitchen. They snagged Mikki along the way.

"What's up?" she said, licking the frosting from an éclair off her fingers.

"That's what I'm wondering," Lauren said. She looked Rory up and down with the keen eye she usually reserved for the subject of one of her articles. "Have you been feeling okay, Rory? I swear you looked positively green during the ribbon-cutting."

"Yeah," Mikki put in. "Nolan and I thought you were going to yak right there on the sidewalk."

Rory patted her stomach. "I've been queasy the past few days, that's all."

"That's *all*?" Lauren asked with a portentous air.

"What are you trying to say?" Rory blurted, but suddenly she knew.

"I'm sure I'm wrong, and this is certainly presumptuous of me to ask, but I just wondered…have you considered that you might be pregnant? You've had a queasy stomach for about a week now."

"Oh, no," Rory heard herself say from a distance.

"'Oh, no, that's not possible' or 'Oh, no, the condom broke'?" Mikki asked.

"Neither. Either. Both." Rory covered her face. "I don't know what I'm saying."

"Let's not jump the gun. You've always had a sensitive stomach. Remember how you couldn't eat for a week when you signed the lease for your first store?"

"Remember how you puked at your bridal shower?" Lauren added. "We should have known then that Brad wasn't the one for you."

Rory opened her mouth, but no words came out. She was backtracking in her head to the mud baths at Painter's Cove resort and how they'd messed around in the shower without a condom. It was impossible to conceive that way. Practically impossible. Of course, condoms were only around ninety percent effective under optimal circumstances, so there was always a chance. She backtracked some more, trying to figure out where she'd been in her cycle.

Mikki patted her arm. "Is your period overdue?"

Rory swallowed, trying to calm the roiling of her

stomach. If she hadn't been nauseous before, she would be now. "Not yet."

"Then we won't worry until it is," Lauren said, but Rory saw the expression on her sister's face as she went to find a kettle and fill it with water. "I'll make you tea and toast. That always settles your stomach."

"I didn't plan this," Rory was compelled to say after an agonizing silence. "I know I've said I want a baby, but I wouldn't intentionally trick Tuck—er, any man into the situation."

"Of course not," Mikki soothed. "You don't need to tell us that. We know you, Rory. You're so fair and honest, Scouts earn Aurora Constable badges."

Rory tried out a weak chuckle, but it did no good for her mood. "Tucker will go ballistic," she muttered, turning to grip the edge of the counter.

Mikki nudged her onto a stool. "I've never seen him have a temper. He's too easygoing."

"Yeah, you're right. You're right." He wouldn't get mad; he'd make a joke or start acting a little dodgy. Not that Rory could blame him. She'd be freaking, too, if she wasn't having trouble remembering to breathe. Nor could she seem to wrap her mind around the idea that she might be pregnant.

By Tucker.

She slumped against the counter with her head in her hands.

"Tea," came Lauren's soft voice, and a cup appeared in front of Rory. She inhaled the herbal steam, reminded of the comforts of home.

Uh-oh. She sat up. *"Mom."*

Lauren's eyes widened. Mikki said, "Bloody hell."

"Go!" Rory ordered them. "Cut her off at the pass. I don't want her back here. You know what she's like. She'll see me, figure out what's wrong with her third eye or something and then probably take it upon herself to announce my 'happy' news to the crowd." Rory pushed her sisters toward the door. "Go. Go now."

Her sisters called out a few reassurances and ran from the kitchen. Didi, Tucker's older sister, stepped aside at the door to let them by.

She approached Rory. "Was it something I said?"

Rory managed to summon up a welcoming smile. "No, those were my sisters. I'd have introduced you, but they're on a mission."

"For more cheesecake?" Didi patted her midriff. "I've tried all the samples and put a 'La Dolce Vita' cheesecake on reserve for home."

"Tell them at the counter that it's yours with my compliments."

"Thanks, but really, that's not necessary. You won't turn a profit that way."

"Now you sound like my mother." Rory glanced warily at the door.

"Are we hiding out?" Didi asked.

"Yep." Rory made a motion to slide off the stool. "Would you like a cup of tea? It's green tea, I'm afraid. More for medicinal purposes than taste, although Lauren knows how to brew it properly so there's no bitterness."

"Let me get it." Rory pointed out the stash of porcelain cups and saucers in assorted flowery patterns and

Didi worked with the efficiency of a mother, at home in any kitchen.

A couple of the workers entered—making Rory jump—but they quickly gathered up armfuls of the signature boxes and sprigs of lavender and departed, assuring her that the store traffic was under control.

Didi joined Rory at the counter. She sipped her tea, quiet for a moment, although it was obvious she was eager to talk.

Rory turned her cup on its saucer. For the moment, her stomach had settled. Her mind—that was still jumpy.

"Mmm. This is not bad. Medicinal, you said?"

Rory had prepared for the question. "I have a touch of a stomach flu."

Didi made comforting sounds. "So that's why you looked kind of rocky out there."

Had *everyone* noticed? Surely not the men. Not Tucker.

"I'm feeling better now."

Luckily, Didi dropped the subject. "I hope you don't mind that I barged in on you like this. But I just had to meet you."

"I was surprised that Tucker agreed for you to go along with him. He's been rather…"

"Secretive?"

"Uh-huh." Rory's old self-esteem issues had risen their ugly heads and whispered that he hadn't wanted to introduce her to his brothers because he was embarrassed—just a little—that she was so different from the typical hot chick they'd probably expect. Not that she expected them to be appalled. They might even prefer her. It was that first moment of amazement that would make her cringe.

"Don't take that to heart," Didi said in a sincere voice that was impossible to disbelieve. "With four brothers and sisters and an equal number of assorted in-laws, our boy Tuck has learned to keep his mouth shut when he's serious about a woman."

Serious. There was still a distracting *I'm-knocked-up* buzz going on in Rory's brain, but she was certain that Didi had said *serious*.

"I, um, I thought that Tucker doesn't do serious."

"That's the reputation."

"Not the reality?"

Didi gave a wry grin. "No, it's the reality, too."

"Oh, well."

"Except that he did allow me to come to your grand opening. That's something." Didi paused. "You're serious about him, aren't you?"

Blaming it on Didi's open friendliness, Rory found herself admitting to the truth. "Yes, I'm afraid I am."

"Aw, there's nothing to be afraid of. Tuck's a good guy."

"That's what everyone says." But Rory wondered if his feet had ever been put to the fire by as serious a situation as a pregnancy scare.

"It's the rest of us you've got to watch out for," Didi said with a merry laugh. "For instance, after Sam and Gabe interrupted you guys last Saturday, Gabe came to me with an outrageous story about Tuck hiding a lover in the bedroom. After the way he'd been so secretive about his weekend in Mendocino, combined with your name being Rory, they jumped to the conclusion that you were a man."

"A man?" Rory broke out in giggles. "You've got to be kidding! How could anyone think Tucker would—" She snorted. "With a man—? Oh, my God."

"My brothers can be dense," Didi said. "But I wasn't taken in for a minute. You're the woman from the key party, aren't you?"

"Yes." Rory's hand went automatically to her neck, but the necklace wasn't there.

"I thought so. Right from the start, Tucker was different about you."

"How so?"

Didi mulled that. "It's hard to say. All I can come up with is that he didn't talk much about you and he never joked. Other girls, he'd tell us about how he'd met this blonde who quoted *Glamour* like Shakespeare, or a tennis pro who bedded the linesmen between matches. We got *nothing* on you."

"Yeah, because I'm no—"

Didi waved her off. "Because he's serious about you."

Rory almost didn't dare to hope that could be true. "You're sure that's why?"

"As sure as a big sister can be."

"I'm a big sister." They shared a smile of understanding.

"Then you know how siblings sometimes need to have their lives arranged for them," Didi said, "and a few little truths pointed out."

They laughed. "I worry about sticking my nose in,"

Rory confessed. "Don't want to be bossy like my mother."

"Oh, gosh, I surpassed my mother years ago." Didi drained her tea and set the cup down with a small crash. "Once you have kids, you'll lose any inhibitions about interfering."

Kids. At that mention, Rory had to strive to maintain a smile. Tuck might be the greatest "good guy" in the world, but an unexpected bundle of joy put the fear in even the best of men.

"SATISFIED?" Tucker said to Didi as they drove away in his work truck, a pickup with his name and phone on the door and his gear stowed in the covered bed.

"Very."

"What did you and Rory talk about when you cornered her in the kitchen?"

"There was no cornering. We had a cup of tea like proper ladies. And a good conversation."

"That's the part that worries me."

"I praised you to the heavens."

"Yeah, sure."

"Okay, I told Rory you're smitten."

"Smitten? For Pete's sake—I'm not a girly man. I don't get smitten."

"Shut up and be glad I didn't say more."

He shut up until they reached the next intersection. Then, tentatively, "Like what?"

Didi pounced. "Like, you're in love with her."

He shut up again. For three blocks, all downhill. If that was a metaphor for the day, he was in trouble.

"What makes you think I'm in love with her?"

"I can read you like a book." Didi became thoughtful. "Do you remember when you were eight? You cherished your baseball glove so much you even cuddled with it in bed at night. You wouldn't let Sam or Gabe touch the thing, especially after they almost lost it in the park. You sobbed as if your heart was broken until Dad went back and found the glove under some bush or other."

"So you're saying Rory is a cheap old baseball glove. I'm sure she'd be thrilled with the comparison. I loved my Hot Wheels race track, too."

Didi plucked the sprig of lavender from the bakery box in her lap and sniffed. "The race track was sold in a garage sale years ago," she said airily, "but where is that old baseball glove?"

"In my bedroom closet," Tucker answered at once, before he realized she'd tricked him.

She put on her smug big-sister smile. "Hmm. Isn't that interesting."

"What of it?" Tucker said grumpily.

"I'll leave that to you to figure out."

He already had it figured out, at least as far as he could. "Seriously, Deeds, what did you think of Rory?"

"I liked her a lot. We bonded."

"She's not my usual girlfriend."

Didi looked askance. "Because she's smart, successful and so real she has no silicone parts?"

"Something like that."

"Rory would be a welcome addition to our family."

"Now, hold on." Tucker braked behind an Alpha

Romero driver who'd decided at the last second that running the yellow light was not a good idea. "We weren't talking about marriage."

"Why not? Rory's perfect for you."

"How can you say that? She's on an entirely different level."

Didi blinked. "What?"

He drummed his fingers on the wheel. "Look, it's obvious, all right? Like you said, she's smart and successful. Cultured, too. She's used to the good things in life. She's destined to marry a doctor or a professor or a...I don't know, newspaper editor, someone with the same outlook and lifestyle. Not a blue-collar guy who lives in a basement apartment."

"Oh, she's a snob, then."

"No, of course not! Did I say that?"

"Sort of. Why are getting so aggravated?"

"Because you're annoying me."

Didi elbowed him. "You're annoying me, too. How you could ever, *ever* put yourself down..." She went off on a five-minute harangue about work ethics and pride and how their parents had raised them to believe in themselves and to be kind and generous to other people no matter what their status. "And that includes the well-off, if you haven't figured it out yet."

"Jeez-us," Tucker said. "Roll back the tongue, Didi. You're not telling me anything I don't know."

Yes, his parents had instilled good values in him. But they'd also raised him in an area dedicated to posher lifestyles than their own. Nolan, as his best friend, had showed him an inside glimpse at how all the money and class in the world didn't necessarily buy a healthy upbringing, but Tucker had always been aware of the trappings that distinguished the haves from the have-nots.

Funny thing, he suspected that Nolan would count the Schulzes as "Haves," in spite of the outward symbols of success that his family had in spades.

Rory, too, he realized.

"Prove that you know it," Didi said.

"How?"

"Ask Rory to marry you."

"It's way too early for that."

"Mumph."

"That's all you have to say?"

"I've rolled my tongue in."

He sighed. "Okay, you have one more shot. Tell me what you're dying to."

Didi wasn't the only one who could read people like books.

She fiddled with the lavender. "This is probably none of my business, and I might be jumping to conclusions as wild as Sam and Gabe—"

"What?"

She waved the sprig. "Oh, never mind that. They were up to their usual shenanigans."

Tucker figured he'd find out. Sooner or later, but definitely at the worst time possible, if his brothers were involved.

"Okay, what's this about Rory? Spill the beans, Didi."

"Yes, boss." She inhaled and spoke in a fast breathless voice. "I overheard her talking with her sisters in the kitchen. And, well, it seems that Rory might be pregnant."

14

ASIDE FROM Garrison Street, Rory had three favorite places to go: her local movie theater, a tumbledown stone B and B she'd discovered in the mountains of the Luberon, and the Ferry Building's farmer's market along the Embarcadero. The movies were for mindless relaxing. The inn was a rare treat. The market—that was for comforting her soul and raising her spirits, a more upscale version of the roadside stands she and Emma used to scour.

But Rory had never been produce-shopping with Tucker at her side. He was being helpful, sweet, attentive—and he was making her jittery.

Or possibly it was the secret. Her maybe-secret.

Her maybe-baby.

"My movie party theme is Italian," she told Tucker as they walked the length of the indoor-outdoor marketplace. The various stalls and storefronts were jammed with tourists and trendy shoppers, but also the usual crush of foodies. She pulled him into her favorite cheese shop. "I need goat cheese and pecorino. But I love their *Fromage Blanc,* so I think I'll get some of that for myself."

"Order as much as you'd like. My treat."

"Don't be silly. It's for my party." She placed an order with the counter person, then pointed out the marvelous red-orange color of the rind on the Red Hawk cheese. "So pretty. Reminds me of sunset in Mendocino."

"We'll go back there someday."

Whoa. Either he was using male code for "Let's get together someday…when the moon turns to cheese" or he was actually putting out feelers for the future.

He took the cheese and paid at the register, brushing off her attempt at protest. "What's next?"

She consulted her list. "Chick peas, pine nuts, fava beans, kale, garlic, roma tomatoes…"

"Are you buying out the market? Good thing I came along."

He'd shown up at her house when she was leaving and invited himself as her escort. When she'd explained about the movie party for her work crew, she'd stumbled over offering him a late invitation, trying to make sure he knew he was wanted all along but that she'd been uncertain about his interest in becoming part of her inner circle. That he'd brought his sister to the opening had changed her mind—sort of—on that count.

She pointed as they passed several busy stalls. "Look at those sweet potatoes. And the Yukon Golds! Scrumptious."

Tucker smiled at her. "You get excited over vegetables like some women do over diamonds."

"Whenever I need to lose, I go on a veggie diet."

"Forget about diets. You're *scrumptious*," he said, making finger quotes and a funny face.

She wrinkled her nose at him, but a spurt of happiness went through her like a shot of vodka. If she hadn't the one little worry, the day would have been perfect.

They shopped their way down her list, adding items at random when the purple-satin skin of an eggplant or a frill of baby radicchio caught her eye. After a quick bite at a Vietnamese restaurant and a longer stop in one of her favorite French gourmet kitchen suppliers, they headed back to the car.

Tucker was laden with packages. Rory carried a string bag of tomatoes and her purse. If she hadn't known there was no reason for him to suspect, she'd have been suspicious of his extreme solicitousness.

"Drinks and appetizers will be at seven," she told him, waylaid by a return of the jitters. She'd tried a bicarbonate of soda the night before, and that had helped. A sign, she'd decided, still clinging to the upset-stomach theory.

"Do I have to come in costume?" He'd mentioned hearing tales of her previous parties from Nolan, who unfortunately hadn't even been around for her infamous *Gladiator* toga bash.

"No, this one's fairly casual. If you have anything Italian, put it on. I've got to warn you, though—it's chick-flick night. We're watching *Under the Tuscan Sun,* mostly because I decided a hot summer night deserves my best Mediterranean canapés."

"I'll suffer through it," he said, giving her a brooding look with his eyes.

She was nervous again, and covered up with cheerfulness. "There's the car!" She swept off her sun hat and tossed it in the back seat before climbing in. "Stow the packages anywhere. All set? Here we go then!"

Tuck reached over and pulled across her seat belt, still looking at her with those serious eyes. "Is there anything you want to tell me?"

A golf ball suddenly appeared in her throat. She shook her head.

"Nothing?" he prodded.

She gulped. The golf ball became a boulder in the pit of her stomach. "Really, Tucker. I have no idea what you mean."

"When you do…" His hand slid along her leg; he squeezed right above her kneecap. "I'm here for you."

He knew! But how?

Not Lauren or Mikki. They wouldn't do that without her knowing, except under extreme circumstances.

His sister, Didi? Could she have overheard Rory's conversation with her sisters? *Of course.*

Which meant Tuck knew nothing for certain. Rather like her.

"Tucker," she said, holding the key in the ignition, "maybe you think you know something, but you don't. No more than I do. So don't be making plans or promises."

That was too harsh. She amended herself. "Not that I don't appreciate your concern. It's just…too early. Y'know?"

He nodded, although how he could follow her rambling jumble of an explanation she couldn't imagine.

Thoughts and images were swirling in her head—Tucker knee-deep in the ocean, holding up a shell; the way his glance had skipped over her the first time they'd met; the way he'd looked at her in his apartment right before he'd attacked her with a kiss; their polite agreement to be friends; their ravenous hunger to be lovers; how he spoke of his family, making her want to be part of it.

He was, as everyone had told her, a good man. If her pregnancy was real, she could have him. Perhaps even as a husband, because he would volunteer to do the right thing, prodded on by his faith and family even when that conflicted with his current lifestyle.

But she didn't want to get him that way.

She had to know that he was in love with *her*, faults and all. Just as she was with him.

TUCKER STOOD in front of the fancy storefront as if he were facing the guillotine. This wasn't the last place he'd ever expected to visit, but it sure as hell had a spot in the bottom ranks.

He reached for the door handle. The things a man would do for the woman he loved….

An hour later he was decked out from head to toe, wincing at the bill the salesclerk had presented to him as if it were a diploma. He gave up his credit card, fully expecting to hear it scream when the clerk ran it through the machine.

He hoped there was wiggle room left under his spending limit.

Next stop: jewelry store.

RORY STOOD AMID her lavender garden, sniffing the air. She'd already snipped basil and bay leaves. All she needed was a couple florets of the lavender. A little went a long way with the strongly flavored plant.

The skirt of her floral cotton sundress drifted against her legs. The dress was an old one, soft with washing. Her closet had contained garments more fashionably Italian, but the dress made her think of sun-drenched skies and fields of lavender and thyme. Spilled wine and dripping gelato, too.

She glanced over her shoulder. Her mother waved from the kitchen window.

The house was a stalwart three stories, a gray-shingle building in the Cow Hollow neighborhood of the Marina. She had a lacquered lavender front door and a snippet of a view of the Golden Gate bridge from her roof. Love and care had been lavished upon the place, and it represented all the good she'd done for herself after Brad's cruel dumping. Mikki sometimes teased her about being as snug as a bug in her home—too snug, being the implication—but Rory had no regrets. Wooden beams and ancient bricks were more reliable than men. And just as responsive.

Or so she'd believed.

"Tuck will be here soon," she said to herself, simply to feel the zing of anticipation in her blood. He had even her house beat for thrills.

But she was torn. Needing to know about the maybe-baby, yet dreading the outcome, either way. Lauren and Mikki had been conspiring since yesterday, debating the pros and cons of their sister's predicament. Finally they'd opted in favor of the face-the-music choice. Minutes ago, each of them had phoned independently of the other to say that she was bringing a pregnancy test to dinner tonight.

Rory couldn't help but grin. They would have rosemary chicken, a tomato tart and pee on a stick.

EMMA WAS SLIDING the skin off the roasted tomatoes and Rory was chopping kale when Mikki and Lauren arrived with their men. They were early—another conspiracy.

Rory wiped her hands on a towel and went to greet them. After admiring how handsome they were in their Italian wear, she sent Nolan and Josh upstairs to the media room, asking them to rearrange the seating around the new plasma-screen TV. Lauren and Mikki followed her to the kitchen.

"How did you get Josh into that striped shirt?" Rory asked. "If you squint your eyes, he looks just like a gondolier."

"Once I knew a gondolier in Firenze," Emma said, making the rest of them share indulgent smirks over the story they'd heard a hundred times. "His name was Antonio, and he had sad dark eyes and Michelangelo curls that tumbled over his forehead." Smiling to herself, Emma swayed in time to a long-ago song. "Antonio sang to me as we floated along the canal beneath the Ponte Vecchio bridge. He had the sweetest voice and quite an expert mouth."

"Mother!" Rory laughed. "You have no sense of

common decency. Most mothers don't talk like that with their daughters around."

"Pity," Emma said. "Society would be better off if only it emulated me."

"Society would be too busy taking bong hits at Dead concerts," Mikki said.

"There you go. All the world's problems solved." Emma sprinkled olive oil she'd steeped in bay leaves over the tomato-filled tart shell.

"Who else is coming to this party?" Lauren asked. Rory suspected she was trying to deflect attention from the brown paper packet tucked under her arm.

"Katya from the store, with her oldest daughter. Roger, my contractor, and his wife. My friends Lucky and Harold. And Tucker."

"I finally get to meet Tucker?" Emma said dryly. "Saints preserve us." Somehow they'd missed each other at the store opening, although Rory guessed that Tucker had been extraordinarily adept at dodging entanglements since it was rare for her mother to miss a chance to give any of their dates the once-twice-thrice-over.

"If you hadn't been so stuck on bossing my counter people, you might have met him," she murmured. And if Lauren and Mikki hadn't stepped in to keep Emma distracted.

Emma smiled with placid confidence. "I will give him my full attention this evening."

Oh, dear. Perhaps that was just as well, Rory decided. Anything to deflect Emma's attention from *her*.

Rory looked up to see that Lauren was wiggling her

eyebrows up and down and giving small nudges with her chin toward the back stairs.

Mikki, never subtle, took the proverbial bull by the horns. "Rory, hon, that dress won't do. Let's go up and find you something sexy to wear."

"Good idea. Mom, if you're finished with the tart, would you mind toasting the baguette slices? Then brush them with garlic? There's a chicken in one oven, but you can use the broiler in the other." During her reno of the house, one of her greater extravagances had been the installation of double industrial ovens. "We've got three canapé spreads—the kale with pine nuts, chick pea puree with lavender and—"

"Never mind, Lauren will help," Emma interrupted too innocently not to be on to them.

Lauren surreptitiously passed the package to Mikki. "Sorry, Mom, I'm needed upstairs on fashion patrol. We'll be ten minutes."

The three of them hurried to the back steps.

Emma's voice stopped them. "She's not pregnant, you know."

They bumped against each other like Keystone Cops. Lauren groaned. Mikki swore. Rory looked at the ceiling and wondered why she'd ever thought she could pull the wool over her mother's third eye.

"How?" Lauren said.

How did you know, how can you tell, how is it that you'll always be three steps ahead of us? Rory thought with affection and frustration. One day soon, Emma would be the world's greatest grandma.

"I know by looking at her." Emma pointed a basted

finger at Rory. "That's a great-sex glow, not a bun-in-the-oven glow. But go on, take your little drugstore test." She waved her hand in dismissal. "I'm only a mother, why should you believe me."

"Do you believe her?" Lauren whispered as they hustled upstairs.

"She's always right." With her mother's pronouncement, Rory had grown even more reluctant about taking the test. Yes, it was too soon, but she'd started to want the maybe-baby. A little girl had formed in her mind's eye, with curly brown hair and chubby cheeks and Tucker's laugh.

"Pffft." Mikki led the way to Rory's bedroom. "She wasn't right the time that she said Johnny Lucci was gonna get me 'in trouble' if I kept sneaking out at night to meet him."

"You did get in trouble, just not the knocked-up kind," Lauren said.

Rory snickered. "Because she only went to second base, not all the way like she bragged."

"How'd you know that?" Mikki tossed her hair. She'd done a Sophia Loren look with a formfitting dress, spike heels and thick mascara and eyeliner. "Didja inherit Mom's intuition, or what?"

"Maybe."

Mikki's heavily penciled brows arched. "Then you should know if you're pregnant or not."

"I thought I was." Rory looked inside the paper bag—two pregnancy kits. "That might have been wishful thinking."

Lauren made a surprised sound. "You *want* a baby?"

"I've always wanted a baby."

"But having one now could really mess up your relationship with Tucker."

"I know." Reluctantly, Rory opened one of the kits and began to read the directions.

"Here," Mikki said, rustling through the contents and handing Rory the stick. She pushed her toward the bathroom. "Just get it over with. The suspense is killing me."

"You seem to know what you're doing."

"I've had a scare or two."

Knowing Mikki and her longtime aversion to motherhood, she'd had to have been seriously frightened. Rory gave her a quick hug before Mikki pulled the door shut on her.

Five minutes later they were sitting on the edge of Rory's queen-size bed, trying not to stare at the test stick laid on the smoked-glass surface of the walnut Art Deco dresser.

Everywhere she looked, Rory saw her pale face reflected back at her. It hadn't occurred to her before that she had so many mirrored and reflective surfaces in her Hollywood glamour bedroom—the sconces, the Venetian glass mirrors, the crystal bottles and mercury glass vases on a mirrored tray beside the bed. Even the drapes had a shimmer; heavy pewter silk hung at the balcony doors like ball gowns.

She clenched her hands between her knees. "Someone talk."

"Lorelei's been acting up," Lauren said, referring to the pseudonym she wrote under on her blog for *Inside*

Out magazine. "She started a flame war on the magazine's message boards."

Mikki nibbled her thumbnail. "Lorelei's *always* in the middle of a flame war."

Lauren smoothed her vintage Audrey-Hepburnesque bouffant checked skirt, reminiscent of *Roman Holiday*. "Then what's new with you?"

"I'm thinking of having a baby. Eventually. Someday. In the future. Maybe."

Rory goggled.

Beep. The alarm on Lauren's watch went off.

"Hold on." Lauren put up a hand, her eyes widening at Mikki. "You're thinking of having a baby?"

"Nolan wants a family. That was always a major problem in our marriage, even when neither of us wanted to face it. Before, I could never see myself as a mother, but now..." Mikki shrugged tightly. "Things have changed."

"Things don't just change," Lauren said.

Rory was smiling. "They do when you're in love."

"I know that," Lauren said, clearly exasperated at her sisters' mutual lapses into starry-eyed la-la land. They'd always said that at least one of them had to maintain a clear head when it came to men, to steer the others away from ogres masquerading as princes. "This isn't fair. I was waiting to tell you about the romantic dinner Josh prepared the other night, and now I have to be take Mikki's place as the cynical one."

"Nah, that's okay," Rory said. "This once, let's all be goony love-struck girls together."

"Sounds good to me." Mikki, in the middle, wound

her arms around them. "I have to be out of my cynical, cotton-pickin' mind to consider having a baby after all those years of swearing I wouldn't." She hugged them a little tighter. "I'm still scared shitless, but I'm not the same person I was five years ago."

Rory squeezed her right back. "You're growing up. You're forgiving your mother for abandoning you."

"You're forgiving *yourself*," Lauren added softly.

"It's a work in progress," Mikki admitted. After a minute of snuffling sister-bonding, she shrugged them off and hopped up. "Okay, sob sisters! Before we break out the tissues for our issues, let's take a look at this test of Rory's and see if we're about to make Emma's day by embarking on a generation of key babies."

The butterflies in Rory's stomach had multiplied times ten. If she opened her mouth, they'd fly out like the plague of locusts in *The Mummy,* so she only looked at Mikki and nodded a go-ahead.

Time to know the truth.

TUCKER ARRIVED to a roomful of people, most of their faces recognizable even if he didn't know their names. Before he could say more than "Hello" and "How are you?" Rory's sisters had him by the arms and were rushing him through the vestibule to the staircase that divided the house.

"Rory's upstairs," they said. "She needed a minute alone. But you should go to her."

Oh, man, he thought, climbing to the second floor. He put his hand in his pocket and felt the weight of the small box the jeweler had provided. *Oh, man. This is it. Has to be.*

"Rory?" he said at the top. Her house was like her— classy and clean, organized, rich, tasteful. But also welcoming and warm, with the aroma of dinner mingling with the scent of the fresh flowers in a big crystal urn. A chandelier illuminated the stairwell and the upper landing.

The bedroom door was open. Rory sat at the foot of the bed. She looked up and saw him, pasting a smile on her face as she shoved the small item she'd been looking at beneath her leg. "Hi."

"Hi." He waited in the doorway.

"Come in." She blinked several times as she took in his appearance. "What *are* you wearing?"

"You said to dress Italian." He indicated the white raw silk shirt. "Prada." The leather belt and caramel-colored trousers with a knife-edge pleat. "Armani." Gleaming dark leather loafers. "Gucci."

Giggles erupted from Rory. "You nut! Josh looks like a gondolier and Nolan came in an Italian soccer jersey. You didn't have to invest so much…effort."

Tuck adjusted one sleeve, previously carefully rolled to the elbow, just so, by the store clerk. "I wanted to show that I can be polished, too."

"You do look very handsome." She patted the bed for him to sit beside her. "But I like you in jeans and a tool belt just as much."

"I wanted to fit in."

"But Josh and Nolan—"

"With *you*," he said.

Ah. "I told you about my granny's-hopsack phase, right? Clothes don't make the person, they only present an image." She caught her own eye in the fancy Venetian mirror over the dresser. Who was she trying to impress? Herself? Long-gone Brad? A vague watercolor idea of some potential mate who'd care more about her style than her heart?

"I'm sorry if I've made you feel that you're not good enough for me," she said. "Because you are. I've never had one moment of doubt about that."

"That's my deal to figure out." He sat.

"The doubts I've had go in more the opposite direction." She blinked at him. "Like, am I good enough for you?"

His expression was disbelieving. "You're kidding me."

She bumped her shoulder against his and gave a little laugh at their dovetailed insecurities. "Then I guess that's *my* deal to figure out."

They went silent for a few moments, digesting the idea of moving forward without the stutter steps of worrying if they should, how they should, and who was watching. Tucker felt that a weight was gone from his shoulders, one he hadn't fully realized he carried.

"I should probably go downstairs," Rory mused.

"Not yet." He took her hand. "There's something I have to say." If she wouldn't go first, he would. There'd be no doubts on this point. "About you and me and making this a permanent arr—"

"Wait." Rory had stiffened. "I have to show you this."

She pulled out the wandlike item she'd been hiding. "You've probably guessed what was up, but, well, this is it—officially. My early pregnancy test." Her thumb was over the small window that showed the results.

He reached for her hand again, but didn't attempt to discern the symbol. "I want you to know that I'm with you, either way."

"That means a lot to me, Tucker." She took a deep breath and showed him the stick. "But it's negative. I'm not expecting."

All he could say was, "Oh."

"No jumping for joy?" she asked, smiling a little. "I'm sure neither of us was ready for a baby."

"Right. I'll be honest. I am relieved. *But...*"

"Yes," she said, her eyes lighting up. "That's how I feel. Relief. *But...*"

He stroked her fingers, one by one, imagining him and her together for a year, a decade, a lifetime. There would be kids, several of them. Maybe they'd even be foster parents. Big families were a pain in the keister, but worth it.

Before that, though, he wanted Rory to himself. Every night he would have her strip for him and be awed once more by the lush beauty and unconscious grace her nudity revealed.

"It's something to consider," he said. "In the future."

"The future. Then we have one?"

An instinctive and extremely non-PC proprietorship rose up inside him. "You know we do."

"I'd hoped, but then...with the way we were so in-decisive at the beginning, about whether to go to

Painter's Cove, whether we should sleep together, then whether we should *stop* sleeping together, et cetera, et cetera." She laughed, lightly but a bit defensively. "You can understand why a girl might get confused."

"Maybe it's just me, but I've never felt like we had a lot of choice in this. I know I've come across as a guy who's not ready to settle down, but that's only because I didn't have a reason to. It's like my brother told me, weeks ago, when I wasn't sure about going away with you. When it's right, it's right. Now I realize that we were going to happen no matter what. You know—" He felt vaguely foolish, but he said it. "Fate."

"Lock and key," she mused. "Except you're forgetting. You swapped keys with another guy."

"Who says it wasn't fated to happen that way?"

Her second laugh was more genuine. "You've got to meet my mother. That's something she'd say."

"I saw her downstairs. Was she the one with the long hair streaked with gray, wearing some kind of robe, very, uh, full-figured?" His hands circled near his chest, making the universal guy sign for big breasts. "She was bearing down on me, but Lauren and Mikki whisked me away upstairs."

Rory nodded. "That's Emma. She's a great believer in fate."

Suddenly he didn't want to talk about Mrs. Constable. Not when he had her daughter alone in a bedroom. He traced a finger over Rory's cheek. "I happen to be a great believer in chemistry."

She pulled a leg up beneath herself, moving in close

with her hands on his chest. "And not just *that* kind," he added, as the test stick fell from her lap.

"The party," she said, kissing him.

"Is up here," he countered, working on the buttons of her dress. He had managed to slip his hand inside to find that she'd worn an extra layer—a slip that still wasn't enough to disguise the rigid bump of her nipple—when she pushed his hand away and jumped to her feet.

"Tuck! We can't. Not with company in the house." Fanning her face, she went to open the balcony door to catch the summer breeze.

Tucker joined her, satisfying his hunger with a hand placed on her bottom. That would do in the short term, he thought, wondering how long these movie parties usually lasted.

"Hey," he said, reminded of his original intention when he looked down the gap in her dress. "I have something for you." He dug in his pocket.

"What is it?"

"You'll see. I stopped at the jeweler's this afternoon. They were able to get this open, but they said making a new key would take a while longer."

Rory inhaled when he flicked open the small box. "My necklace." She made a tentative reach for it, then stopped. "Do I get it back? Wasn't there going to be some sort of challenge involved?"

He winked. "Not this time."

She twined the chain around her fingers and dangled the locket between them. "Thank you. I've felt incomplete without it."

"Look inside," he said before realizing that the tiny suitcase had snapped shut. "Damn. It's locked again."

"I have the key," she blurted. She handed him the necklace and disappeared inside for a few moments before returning with the miniature key pinched between finger and thumb. "I kept the key from the party. I tried to tell you once, when we were on our way home from Mendocino, but then you distracted me."

"Or vice versa."

"What did you do with this?" she wondered, inserting the key. The suitcase sprang open and she gasped in delight over his surprise.

She'd brought a digital camera on their trip up the coast and over the course of the weekend had asked various passers-by to snap their photo, then shared them with him in e-mails. He had fitted his favorite into the locket. The shot was one of them seated in her convertible, smiling at each other, the ocean breeze in their hair.

"It's a perfect choice for the suitcase locket," Rory said, peering inside. "We look so adventurous."

"That's what I thought." He glanced over the garden below, noticing for the first time the stalks of lavender rippling in the lazy breeze. Life was good. Damn good.

A cat brushed against his trouser leg, moving in and out of a patch of sunshine that lay on the stone pavers of the balcony. "Hey, Bogey," Rory said, picking up the fat tabby and handing it to Tucker. "This is Bogey. Bacall must be close by. They're always together."

He petted the purring cat, then let it jump down when it meowed as its mate appeared on the balcony.

He gathered Rory into his arms instead and held her soft body tight against his chest. She sighed with pleasure and found his waiting lips.

"This is how it's meant to be," he eventually whispered into her ear. "You and me, Rory, together on the adventure of a lifetime."

HARLEQUIN® *Blaze*™

If you loved her story
GOOD TIME GIRL,
you'll go crazy for

THE COWBOY WAY
by **Candace Schuler**
Blaze #177

Jo Beth Jensen is practical. Burned once by a
cowboy, she swore never to get involved with another
one. But sexy Clay Madison is different. A champion
rodeo bull rider, Clay is just too easy on the eyes to
ignore. Although she knows she should steer clear,
Jo Beth can't help herself. Her body needs some sexual
relief, and the cowboy way is the only way to go....

Available April 2005.
On sale at your favorite retail outlet.

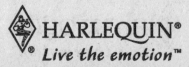

HARLEQUIN®
Live the emotion™

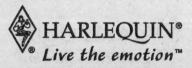

If you enjoyed what you just read,
then we've got an offer you can't resist!

Take 2 bestselling
love stories FREE!
Plus get a FREE surprise gift!

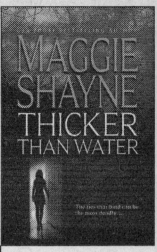

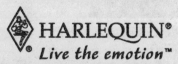